BLOOD EAGLE

A Novel

Roy A. Teel Jr.

BLOOD EAGLE

A Novel

Roy A. Teel Jr.

The Iron Eagle Series: Book Twenty-Five

NARROWAY
PRESS

An Imprint of Narroway Publishing LLC.

Narroway Publishing LLC.
Imprint: Narroway Press
P.O. Box 1431
Lake Arrowhead, California 92352

This is a work of fiction. Names, characters, places, and incidents either are the product of the author's imagination or are used fictitiously, and any resemblance to actual persons, living or dead, business establishments, events or locales is entirely coincidental.

First Edition

Hardcover: ISBN: 978-1-943107-42-1

Teel, Roy A., 1965-
    Blood Eagle: A Novel, The Iron Eagle Series: Book Twenty-Five /
    Roy A. Teel Jr. – 1st ed. – Lake Arrowhead, Calif.: Narroway Press,
    c2020. p.; cm. ISBN: 978-1-943107-42-1 (Hardcover)

1. Hard-Boiled – Fiction. 2. Police, FBI – Fiction. 3. Murder – Fiction. 4. Serial Killers – Fiction.
5. Mystery – Fiction. 6. Suspense – Fiction. 7. Graphic Violence – Fiction. 8. Graphic Sex – Fiction.
9. Thriller – Fiction.
I. Title.

    Book Editing: Finesse Writing and Editing LLC
    Cover and Book Design: Priceless Digital Media
    Author Photo: Z

For Jay

Also by Roy A. Teel Jr.

Nonfiction:

*The Way, The Truth, and The Lies: How the Gospels
Mislead Christians about Jesus' True Message*

*Against the Grain: The American Mega-church
and its Culture of Control*

Fiction:

The Light of Darkness: Dialogues in Death: Collected Short Stories

And God Laughed, A Novel

The Plane Trip: A Short Story

The Savior: A Short Story

The Iron Eagle Novel Series:

Rise of The Iron Eagle: Book One

Evil and the Details: Book Two

Rome Is Burning: Book Three

Operation Red Alert: Book Four

A Model for Murder: Book Five

Devil's Chair: Book Six

Death's Valley: Book Seven

Cleansing: Book Eight

Rampage: Book Nine

Dark Canyon: Book Ten

Deliverance: Book Eleven

Phoenix: Book Twelve

Pray: Book Thirteen

Equality of Mercy: Book Fourteen

Metro: Book Fifteen

Reaper: Book Sixteen

Encryption: Book Seventeen

Selfie: Book Eighteen

Suffering: Book Nineteen

Ransom: Book Twenty

Middlemen: Book Twenty-One

Suburban: Book Twenty-Two

Masquerade: Book Twenty-Three

Anthem: Book Twenty-Four

"There are two kinds of serial killers as far as the victim is concerned: the kind that you don't see before they pounce on you and the kind you see and don't expect to pounce on you."

—Pat Brown

"What does signature mean? Supposedly these are the added touches that make the crime personal to the killer."

—Pat Brown

ſEAL OF THE IRON EAGLE™

Table of Contents

Chapter One 1

Chapter Two 9

Chapter Three 22

Chapter Four 28

Chapter Five 40

Chapter Six 49

Chapter Seven 63

Chapter Eight 74

Chapter Nine 82

Chapter Ten 93

Chapter Eleven 100

Chapter Twelve 109

Chapter Thirteen 120

Chapter Fourteen 130

Chapter Fifteen 144

Chapter Sixteen 153

Chapter Seventeen 161

Chapter Eighteen 176

Chapter Nineteen 182

Chapter Twenty 187

Comforter 192

About the Author 199

CHAPTER ONE

"What the hell happened to his face, chest, and groin?"

Jade had asked Jim and Sam to come to the crime scene at the downtown branch of the Los Angeles Public Library. Jessica was still reeling from what she had seen, but Jim took one look at the body face down in the bushes and said, "Blood eagle. One hell of a brutal and agonizing way to die."

"Blood eagle? That's a Viking myth."

"Well, Jade, it might have been a myth five minutes ago, but it's real now. Those aren't wings on that guy's back. They're his ribs, spread eagle, and his lungs were pulled out of his body backward. It's one of the most gruesome ways to die, and you don't die right away either. It can take days under the right circumstances. Someone hated this guy, and this manner of murder makes the Iron Eagle's methods seem kind. Whoever did this had some powerful tools or was really, really strong. Have you flipped him over yet?"

"No."

"Well, given the fact that the streets are teaming with onlookers, you might want to get the full scope of this killing."

Jade had two workers move the body to the walkway where they flipped him over. Sam covered her mouth, and Jessica and Jade both recoiled. Jim leaned down, staring hard at what remained of the man's body, then pulled a cigarette out of his top left pocket, lit it, then took a photo with his tablet and hit send.

"What the hell are you doing?" Jade asked.

"I've seen this before. So has John. I just emailed the picture to him."

"For what fuckin' purpose, Jim? This is LAPD's case. It's my case."

"That remains to be seen. We don't know who the victim is yet. Any idea on how long he's been dead?"

"Body temp is in the mid-eighties. The night was cool, so I'm guessing he died between three and eight a.m."

"Jesus Christ!" Sam said. "What the hell happened to his face, chest, and groin?"

"He was shaved down," Jim said. "Have you ever used a mandoline when cooking? They're razor sharp. That's what happened to this guy. He was run slowly and methodically over the same type of tool. Jade, you'll most likely find ligature marks on the arms and thighs. That's how he was held in whatever type of unit this killer used. I would say that our killer has experience in butchering as well as torturing his prey. This took hours, and this guy felt the cut of every blade, but that didn't kill him."

Jade looked at Jim and asked, "Are you a medical examiner now?"

"Nope." He took a deep hit off his cigarette. "I know how this type of torture works. The cause of death will be suffocation. It's really fuckin' hard to breathe when your lungs have been pulled through your back."

>———<⦿>———<

John was working on reports when the photograph came over on his tablet. He looked at it and called Jim and asked, "Where are you?"

"Los Angeles Public Library. The main branch on Fifth."

"Any ID on the victim?"

"Not yet. What you see is what we know. Does that photograph bring back any memories?"

"Yes ... blood eagle. There haven't been any cases in at least a decade."

"Do you remember the last case?"

"Of course, I remember. Lester Black. Nineteen ninety-eight. Founder of Black Robotics. Found slain the same way."

"As I recall, Black was working for the Defense Department at the time of his murder."

"That's right."

"And you worked the case as a street detective for LAPD before moving over to the Bureau when the case was suddenly closed by Steve Hoffman and the director. They killed the case and filed it under cold cases as I recall."

"What are you getting at, Jim?"

"It's not a cold case anymore, John. I have five bucks that says this guy is a part of the Black family and that someone is testing a new robot."

"I can't jump into this case right now, Jim, and you know that. I need an ID and then I can work from there."

Jim held the phone away from his ear. "Has this scene been cleared? Is there any identifying information on the victim?" Jade shook her head. "No ID out here. I guess Jade and Jessica will have to do their magic."

"Ask Jade to check the mouth for teeth." Jim did as John asked, and Jade leaned over the body and pulled the mouth open.

"Jesus, Jim! They've all been removed."

"No teeth, John. Starting to come into focus?"

"Which members of Lester's family were still alive after his murder?"

"He had a son. Steven Black. He was fifteen when his father was murdered and as I recall he had some type of mental problem."

"He had a half-sister who was five years older than him, too. I'll need to pull the file to find her name."

"As I recall, she had nothing to do with the family. She was from Lester's first marriage, and they weren't on good terms."

"I remember. You need to follow up on Steven Black to see if he's involved with his father's company. You should also find out what Black Robotics is doing these days. Once you have more answers, let me know."

"Will do." Jim paused briefly, then said, "John, whoever killed this guy didn't like him at all. This makes the Eagle's killings look tame."

"Yeah. Unsettling, isn't it?"

"You're of Norwegian descent, aren't you John?"

"Yes, so what?"

"I remember you mentioning being a descendant of Leif Erickson."

"Where are you going with this, Jim?"

"Just drilling for the nerve, John. Just drilling for the nerve."

"Don't go down that road with me."

"I'm just saying you're a descendant of some of the first Vikings. Your father and mother still have their family home in Iceland. You might want to brush up on Norse history because from all of my recollections this type of killing started with them, pal." Jim hung up the line, and Jade asked if John was coming, but Jim told her John wanted a positive ID on the victim first.

"That's not going to be easy. I can't use dental records. I can use genetics if the guy is in the database, but this is going to take some time."

"I have some possible leads here as well. Who found the body?"

"The head librarian. Joanne Fontaine. She's in her office being calmed down and debriefed."

"Okay, well, you take care of the carcass, and Sam and I will speak with Ms. Fontaine."

Jessica sneered at Jim. "Show a little respect, Jim. A man has been savagely murdered."

"Respect? I thought I was. You two bag the guy up. Geez, what a mess."

"What's up?" Chris asked after receiving John's page to come to his office. John handed him his tablet with the crime scene photo, and Chris exclaimed, "Jesus! What the fuck happened to this poor bastard? Is it a man or a woman?"

"A man. He was mandolined and then blood eagled."

"Blood eagled? I thought that was a myth."

"It's no myth. I've only seen it one other time in my career and that was nearly two decades ago."

"And that was an unsolved case?"

"Yes."

"Is this our case?"

"Not yet, but I have a strong feeling it's going to be."

"So, what now?"

"We wait for Jim and Jade to ID the victim, then we'll know how to proceed."

Joanne was sitting at her desk flanked by two LAPD detectives. Jim and Sam walked in, and Jim was about to introduce himself when one of the detectives asked, "What the hell are you doing here, O'Brian? Sam's the Sheriff, not you."

"Jesus, Bill. That's some type of welcome. You know my position with the Sheriff's Department."

"It's LAPD's case."

Sam interrupted, "It's LAPD's case until I say it isn't, got it?"

The two detectives looked at each other, and Bill said, "You two do whatever the fuck you want. Ms. Fontaine is obviously very upset, so be nice."

"Bill, when have you known me not to be nice?"

"I wasn't talking to you, Sheriff. I was talking to O'Brian."

"Jesus, you people treat me like I'm the plague."

Bill pointed to the office exit, and he and his partner started for it. Just before leaving, he turned back to Jim and said, "No, Jim. We can get rid of the plague. You're more like an antibiotic resistant flesh-eating bacteria. Once you get under someone's skin, they feel like they need to chop off the limb."

Jim looked at Sam who shrugged and said, "It's true." Jim nodded as the two left.

Joanne was sipping coffee as the dialogue went on around her. When the two detectives had left, Sam handed Joann her card as well as Jim's then asked about the body. Jim sat silent, and the two women spoke of Joanne's trauma upon finding the body. Sam was sympathetic, and she asked Joanne if there had been any unusual activity at the library in recent days or weeks.

"No, Sheriff. Nothing that stands out. I had the monthly meeting of the city and county librarians here last night. There was nothing out of the ordinary. I have regulars who come to the library often, and I have a few that come daily. I have been here for two decades, so I get to know everyone pretty well. There has been nothing out of the ordinary at all."

Sam asked, "Ms. Fontaine, you stated that you have people who come to the library regularly?"

"About a half dozen come in every day and read. Most are retired and enjoy the library as well as the hustle and bustle of downtown."

"And you know these people by name?"

"Of course. I make it a point to know all of my regulars."

"What time does the library open?"

Joanne looked up at the large clock on the wall in her office. "Nine thirty. I'm sure that my assistants have started to let people in at the main entrance, so long as LAPD has allowed it."

Jim spoke up, "LAPD will allow it. Let's take a walk, and you can introduce us to your regulars." Joanne walked the two out into the main library. There was a small gathering near the entrance, and she walked up and spoke to each one and then introduced Sam and Jim. She introduced each person by first and last name, and Jim was doing a head count and said, "I count five. I thought you had six?"

"Indeed. Has anyone seen Steven?" she asked.

"Steven who, Ms. Fontaine?"

"Black. Mr. Steven Black. He's here seven days a week. Has anyone seen him this morning?" No one spoke up. They just shook their heads.

"Mr. Black," Jim paused, "is he in his early forties?"

"Yes."

"Do you know anything about him?"

"He's had a huge crush on me for years and has asked me out many times, but I refused him."

"Why is that?"

"That's personal, Mr. O'Brian."

"There is a dead body being hauled away from the side entrance to your library, Ms. Fontaine, a body that you found. Right now that's what I'm concerned with, so I'm sorry if you find my questions intrusive, but they may be relevant."

"I'm celibate, Mr. O'Brian. I don't date and never have. That isn't going to change. Mr. Black is not a forward person. He just made it clear that he liked me and wanted to date, and I put off his advances for years."

"Do you know what Mr. Black does for a living?"

"I learned just yesterday that he receives money from a trust fund from a family business. I don't know if he has a formal diagnosis, but I think that he has some form of high functioning autism. He's a brilliant mind but not a very social person; he's a bit awkward."

"Awkward?"

"He doesn't seem comfortable around people."

"But he asked you out on multiple occasions?"

"Yes, sir."

"This trust fund … do you know anything about it?"

"Not really. He told me he inherited the company after his father's death nearly two decades ago and that he doesn't get involved in the operations."

"Did he give you the company name?"

"Black Robotics and AI, I believe. He didn't get into what they do; he just let me know he had money."

Jim pointed to the front exit, "Sam, a moment." The two left the building, and Jim pulled a cigarette out of his top left pocket, lit it, and snapped his Zippo shut. "I know who our victim is."

"Really? You asked a librarian a few questions, and you know who our victim is?"

"Yeah. Let's get the fuck out of here and over to Jade's office."

"Don't you think we should ask a few more questions, perhaps wait and see if Mr. Black shows up?"

"Steven Black has already shown up, and Jade and Jessica have him in their van. Now, let's stop wasting time. You have no idea what we're dealing with."

Sam stepped back inside and thanked Joanne as well as the others and passed out her cards to them. "If Mr. Black shows up, please call my cellphone." They all nodded as Sam left the building.

Jim was on his cellphone, pacing and smoking when she returned. "The dead guy is Steven Black, John. Jade and Jessica have carted his torn apart remains to the morgue."

"How can you be so sure?"

"Just meet us at Jade's office. I know the killer didn't expect us to figure out who the victim was so fast. I mean, you only mutilate a body this meticulously to make identification difficult because you need time."

"Time for what?"

"That's the million-dollar question, John."

CHAPTER TWO

"Oh God! What's happening?"

"It's like walking amongst angels." A gloved hand ran across the dead and dying hanging by special brackets attached to their backs. There were gasps and groans from those alive, light steam rose from both their open backs and their short breaths as the victims tried to breath in the temperature-controlled room. A weak female voice could be heard praying, and her captor walked to her and looked up at the pretty young face. "That's a beautiful prayer, Kristy. Did you learn that at church?"

"Who are you? Why are you doing this to me?"

"Oh, well, that's a hard question to answer. There really is no easy answer. I can tell you that had your mother been nicer to me and helped me out when I needed it, you wouldn't be here, and this wouldn't be happening to you. But she didn't." The woman ran a gloved hand across Kristy's back and exposed ribs. "I just opened you up this morning. You have days to enjoy this room. I will be having you removed for some cosmetic work on your front side. You know what? You're small enough. What? Are you fifteen now?"

Kristy nodded weakly as her assailant grabbed her small legs and lifted her off the hook and dropped her to the floor. There was a bucket of water and several poles with sponges on them, and her attacker grabbed one, dunked it in the water, and started rubbing it all over Kristy's back and lungs. The young girl screamed in agony as best she could given she could take only small breaths.

"Salt water. It adds a bit more pain to the wound. Let's take you out and put you on the table."

The assailant dragged Kristy into another room. Her legs were bound together at the ankles, and her wrists were bound behind her back. Her attacker lifted her onto a table that sat in front of a long conveyor belt. "You have a really nice body for your age, Kristy. I'm not going to lie to you. Things are going to really, really start hurting in a few minutes, and I have to make sure that you feel every cut of the blades, so I need to set an IV."

Kristy tried to resist, but it was hopeless, and once the IV had been set, a large machine moved over the table then lowered over her. There were four white plastic paddles: two on her right and left forearms and two at her calves. The killer made some adjustments as the paddles moved back and forth with a laser sight over her back until they were in position. "Okay, you're going to feel some cold as the IV enters your blood."

The killer started the IV drip, and Kristy became more alert and animated. "What's happening? Oh God! What's happening?"

"Your breathing is better. I just gave you a powerful stimulant. Now, you're going to feel a little pinch on your arms and legs, so hold still."

There was a light laugh, and the machine closed around Kristy's body. There was a loud pop, and the young girl screamed as the machine lifted her and began to move her across from the table to the belt.

"You're really going to love this. I have programed the robot to shave you ever so thin. So thin in fact that your nipples will be the first things shaved off. I will decide how deep I want to go today, but those big tits should shave off over several hours."

The machine began moving her body across the belt until she could see several thin steel blades. "Oh God! What are you doing to me?"

"You might as well relax, Kristy. The next several hours will be gruesome and painful."

The machine jerked back and then forward, and as it did, it slowly lowered Kristy's body over the blades. She let out a scream with the first cuts as the machine gently pressed her body over the blades.

"Look at how thin that meat is! Deli thin, Kristy. Perfect for the dogs."

Kristy howled as the machine lowered and ran her body across the blades, and after several passes the assailant opened a doggy door, and three large Dobermans ran into the room and sat right under the table. They growled at each other as they fought over the meat from Kristy's body. "Didn't I tell you they were going to love you? Well, let's keep going. The boys are very, very hungry."

Jade and Jessica had gotten the body back to the morgue only to find John and Chris waiting for them. "Let me guess. You know who this is?" Jade said coldly.

John nodded. "Jim does, and I fear he is right."

"Well, there are no prints. His hands and feet were soaked in acid; the teeth are gone, and we have taken a blood sample but that could take weeks." John pulled his tablet out along with a small plastic card. He slid the card into a slot on the tablet and asked for a small sample of blood. "What are you going to do with that? Check his blood sugar?" Jade asked.

"No. It's a new state of the art genetic marker identifier."

"I have never seen anything like that before. When did the FDA approve it?"

"I just got my hands on a test model through Sara. Her lab has been allowed to test the mobile units. They have multiple applications for use with infections, influenza, and other maladies."

"Let me guess. This one is set up to do bio markers and DNA?"

"Yes. I have the DNA of the person whom I believe is the victim's father loaded. The unit will cross check markers, and we will have a reading in sixty seconds."

Jessica was pulling a vial of the victim's blood and handed it to Jade. "What the fuck? The feds get their hands on this technology before we do?" Jessica asked.

"No. Sara has had these units for a few months, and Chris and I got one and have been playing with it with Sandy at the Bureau."

"This is known to the Bureau?" Jade asked.

"It's off the record research that Sandy has been doing for us." Jade handed the syringe to John, who put a few drops on the card and stood back looking at the screen on his tablet.

"How will we know if we have a match?" asked Jade.

"It's simple. A green light is a match; a red light isn't."

"No detailed reports or breakdown?"

"My tablet is sending the data back to the lab where Sandy will get a detailed report."

"A report that's not admissible in court, though."

"I don't want it for court, Jade. I want it for myself. A killer like this will never see the inside of a court room."

Jade was about to speak when the light shined green. John lowered his head, and Jessica saw it right away.

"What's wrong, John?"

"The body you have here is that of Mr. Steven Black, the son of Lester Black, the late founder of Black Robotics and AI."

"Black Robotics? The company that is working with the government on AI in robots?" Jade asked.

John nodded and called Jim and said, "I'm at the morgue with Jade and Jess as well as Chris. I just tested the victim's blood. It's positive as a DNA match with Lester Black."

"So, after nearly two decades the killer strikes again?"

"It would appear that way."

"Well, it's your goddamn case now, John. We'll pull it from LAPD unless Black is out of the robotics game with the government."

"No. They're still in it. I just don't know how deep the ties go."

"I'd start making calls if I were you. This killer popped up for a few short weeks nearly two decades ago and then disappeared, now he's back and taking out government contractors. Do you have any idea what the kid's role was with the company?"

"Not yet. I couldn't start digging into it until I had an ID. Now, I do, and I have to walk a damn tight rope. Was Steven Black his only target or are there others? If Black was his only target, we'll never see the killer again."

"And if he's not the only target?"

"Then it's a race against time. He'll most likely be killing even as we speak. We need local missing persons cases."

"Okay. Those don't come in every fuckin' hour, so can you be more specific?"

"Federal employees with missing persons, husbands, wives, kids. I'll have Chris run the databases at the Bureau. I need you and Sam to run county, and I need you to get someone inside the LAPD to run the city."

"John, it's most likely a federal issue. I think you can narrow down the list by checking there first."

"The desperate use all available sources from law enforcement to social media. Let's get it together. We either have a person with a single grudge with the Blacks, or we have something much larger."

Liz Yates arrived at her U.S. Secret Service office just before five a.m. She had been working on an advance team for several senators coming to Los Angeles as well as a late month trip planned by President Hernandez for a fundraiser in several high-profile locations around LA. She was just about to take an early lunch when her cellphone rang.

"Is this Liz Yates with the U.S. Secret Service?"

"Yes, it is."

"Ms. Yates, have you spoken to your daughter this morning?"

"What are you talking about? What about my daughter?"

"I asked a simple question. Have you spoken to Kristy this morning?"

Liz was getting agitated. "I left my daughter safe in her bed this morning. Who the hell is this?"

"Just a concerned citizen. Ms. Yates, your daughter isn't safe at home. That I can assure you."

"Who are you? What's going on with my daughter?"

"I can tell you that she's not fine. She's actually in great agony, Liz. She's paying for your sins."

"Who the fuck is this? Where's my daughter?"

"Don't worry. Kristy will be home in bed when you get there, but she will not be the same as when you last saw her. She is such a little angel. She sure likes to pray, even when in great agony." Liz fumbled through her desk for a hand recorder to try and plug into the phone. "I see our time is up. I don't want you recording my voice. I'm going to leave you a list of your sins. Your angel Kristy paid the price for them for you. I haven't decided if I'm going to come after you or not. I think leaving you to suffer the pains of hell over Kristy is a good start; however, if I change my mind, I will pay you a visit."

The phone line went dead, and Liz grabbed her office phone and made a frantic 9-1-1 call asking police to get to her home. She also called the Secret Service police division and asked them to send a car out to her home as she ran out the front of the building to her car.

It was ten after twelve, and John and Chris had some sandwiches brought in as they went over missing persons cases. Chris had just taken a bite when the office phone rang. John waved him off and grabbed it.

"Swenson."

"John, it's Phil Bailey with the Secret Service."

"Hi Phil. What's up?"

"We have a situation with one of our field supervisors, well, her daughter."

"Okay … do you want to tell me about it?"

"We need you out here at her home right now."

"Do I need a team?"

"Yes, but this needs to be kept covert."

"What the hell is going on, Phil?"

"We have a brutal homicide out here. A senior agents' daughter. Her body has been discovered in her bedroom."

"Give me the address. Have you rolled Jade and Jessica yet?"

"Not yet. I wanted you to see the scene before we started getting others involved."

"What about Jim?"

"No. There'd be an oil and water situation out here if he shows up."

"Who's the victim?"

"Kristy Yates."

"Liz Yates' daughter?"

"Yes, John. It's gruesome. We need you here ASAP. The scene will speak for itself."

"Okay. Text me the address, and Chris and I will be on our way." John hung up the phone as the text came over. "You might want to eat that sandwich fast, Chris."

"Why? What's up?"

"I don't know, but that was Phil Bailey with the Secret Service police force. His boss's daughter has just been found dead in her bedroom. From what Phil told me, it's gruesome."

Chris dropped the sandwich back into its wrapper and rolled it up. He followed John out of the office while asking, "Where are we going?"

"Beverly Hills."

"A Secret Service agent has that kind of money?"

"The agent's name is Liz Yates. She's the heir to the Yates Foundry empire."

"The company that works with the Department of Printing and Engraving?"

"Yeah. It's a small part of their business. They are big into steel and aluminum as well as recycling. It's a huge business with offices around the world."

The two men arrived at the Yates home a half hour later. There were only a few cars and an SUV parked in front of the home, and Chris asked, "This is a homicide scene?"

John nodded as he parked the truck, and the two men got out. Phil met them at the front door. "How many people are on scene, Phil?"

"A handful."

"Where is Liz?"

"We have her sedated in her bedroom. John, she found Kristy after a disturbing phone call at her office."

"Well, lead us to the scene."

John and Chris followed Phil up a large circular staircase and down a brightly lit hall to a room at the end. The smell assaulted all of their senses as they entered Kristy's bedroom and when Chris saw the young girl he turned and vomited over an open railing. John shook his head. Kristy's body had been anchored into the ceiling of her bedroom. She was posed like an angel with her hands placed palm to palm in front of her tortured body. Her head was facing down as if in prayer. Her back had been broken and her ribs spread back and her lungs pulled through the holes. Her bed was covered in blood, and her entire front side had been shaved off down to the abdomen. Her core abdominal muscles were showing, but her internal organs appeared untouched. Her hair was neatly brushed, and John examined the corpse carefully, taking pictures with his tablet. Chris had gotten his composure and reentered the bedroom.

"Who would do something like this to a child, John?" Phil asked.

"Someone very, very sick and or very, very angry." John put a pair of gloves on and felt around the lungs for several minutes and then pulled his hands back, looked at the men in the room, and said, "She's still alive." All faces shuddered, and Phil ran toward the girl, but John pushed him back. "She's been sedated, most likely so that Liz would find her and watch her take her last breath."

"Jesus! We need to cut her down and get an ambulance here," Phil said pleadingly.

John looked at how Kristy's body was suspended and then at the blood on the bed. "If we don't move her correctly, she will die immediately. Her body is booby trapped."

"What do you mean?"

"The child is dead for all intents and purposes. The cables holding her up are attached at her left and right lung and are applying pressure to help keep the airway open, so she is taking shallow breaths. If we release them, her lungs will collapse, and she will die immediately."

"We can't just let her hang here and die."

John walked the room looking at Kristy. Phil and Chris looked on. John pulled out his cellphone and called Sara and said, "I have a fifteen-year-old girl who has been blood eagled but is still alive. She has been hung with cable through her right and left lungs and sedated to allow her to breathe. She has serious trauma to both the front and back of her body. I believe that we might be able to save her, but it is going to require you, Jade, and Jessica as well as me and Chris and some others on scene."

"Give me the address, and I will get to you with an ambulance right away."

"I'm texting it now. You're going to need ICU quality respiratory equipment and blood for her."

"Who else is there?"

"Only a few men and the mother, who has been sedated."

"How is her heart rate?"

John took ahold of Kristy's wrist very gently and looked down at his watch. "Forty-four bpm."

"Do you have any atropine?" John said yes, and Sara responded. "When you hear the sirens on the ambulance, inject the girl with

0.5 milligrams. That will raise her pulse rate. Usually that would be done through an IV push, but you won't have that, but once we are on scene, we can set a line."

"I don't know that she will survive it, Sara."

"Would you rather have her die while we're trying to save her life or let her die a long-suffering death? If she has been blood eagled, there's a chance we can put her back together depending on how she was tortured. The whole idea behind the blood eagle is to keep the victims alive and suffering for days."

"She has severe trauma to her front side. She's been mandolined, and the bulk of her skin has been removed."

"I'm on my way. Call Jade and Jessica."

John hung up the line and told Chris, "Go out to my truck and pull a vial of atropine and a couple of syringes from my bag and bring them in here."

Phil and the other men looked on, and Phil asked, "What the fuck are you doing, John?"

"Trying really, really hard to save this poor girl's life."

"Why do you have atropine in your truck?"

"Do you carry an EpiPen in your car?"

"Of course."

"I carry some medications for emergencies as well, Phil, and atropine is a very common medication to help raise low heart rates. Now, here's the deal. My wife is en route with a paramedic unit. I'm going to call Jade Morgan and Jessica Holmes as we will need their assistance."

"You are going to have the coroner come to the scene of a living person?"

"Yes. Keep your men right here. I will need them to act as soon as the ambulance gets here. We're only going to get one shot at keeping this kid alive, and we all have to work together."

Sara and the ambulance arrived, and John pushed the atropine as instructed. Jade and Jessica were now in the room as were all of Phil's men and the EMTs. Sara hooked Kristy up to an EKG machine and put her on oxygen then checked her vitals and said, "If we are going to do this, now is the time."

John had ahold of Kristy's face and had her head held back to allow air to more easily get in. "On three, you two men cut the cords holding Kristy up. Chris, take her legs and pull them forward. The EMTs will then flip her in midair onto her stomach and then onto the gurney. Jade and Jessica, you two keep the lungs functioning along with Sara on the way to the hospital. Sara, do you have an operating room standing by?"

"Yes, John, along with the best trauma team I have."

John said to Jade, "You're looking at a reverse autopsy, Jade. Do you think we have a chance of keeping this kid alive?"

"The lungs are pink; her skin is pink. She is getting plenty of oxygen. The ribs are spread evenly open to her back. As long as we get her gently onto the gurney and to the hospital, I give her a fifty-fifty chance of survival."

Jessica nodded, and John gave the orders. In a matter of minutes, Kristy's body was out of the house and on the way to Northridge Hospital. Phil and his men had tears in their eyes as they looked around the room. John looked at Chris and Phil then said, "This is still a homicide scene, people, so, let's treat it like one."

Phil asked John, "Do you want me to tell Liz what's going on?"

John paced the large room away from where Kristy's body had been. "Shit, Phil. If we tell her and her daughter dies, she is going to be livid."

"And if we don't tell her, do you think she'll be any less furious?"

"I suppose not. Let's go see her. Chris, work with Phil's men to seal off the bedroom and collect evidence."

"Is this our case, John?"

"A federal employee's child was tortured and possibly murdered, so yeah, it's our case. You men secure the scene while we speak to Liz."

John and Phil walked into Liz's bedroom. She was laying on her bed, propped up on some pillows, half out of it. "Who the fuck would do something like that to my baby, John?"

"I don't know, Liz, but I will find them."

"Jesus Christ! The caller told me that Kristy was praying while the animal tortured her."

"Liz, Kristy is on the way to the hospital."

"What do you mean? She's dead."

"No, she's not. At least she wasn't when she left here. Sara has her, and she is being rushed into surgery as we speak."

"But how could she still be alive?"

"It's a complicated thing to answer right now, and I know you want to get to the hospital, but I have a few house cleaning things I need your help with first."

"Like what?"

"Who called you to tell you about Kristy?"

"A woman. She was soft spoken yet creepy. She told me that she had Kristy but that she was going to be back in her bed."

"When was the last time you saw Kristy?"

"Yesterday morning about four-thirty a.m. I needed to get to the office early to get ahead of some paperwork, and she was sleeping."

"You didn't see her last night or this morning?"

"No. We passed each other. She had school projects and activities, and I had a date and work. So, we didn't see each other last night." Liz paused, "And I didn't look in on her before I left the house this morning. John, I didn't check on her this morning. I was in such a rush to get to the office I just ran out the door. I didn't check on my baby."

"Water under the bridge for the moment, Liz. Did you recognize the caller's voice?"

"No. She said that Kristy was praying, and she taunted me. She knew me, though. She told me that Kristy was paying for my sins."

"Any specifics to your sins?"

"Nothing. She just taunted me then hung up, and I called 9-1-1 and got my men, and we came home."

"Have you had any issues with anyone recently who might want to hurt you or your daughter?"

"Not that I can think of. I mean, I'm working with advance teams from Washington who are getting ready for a congressional visit next week and then the President's advance men for his fundraising visit the end of the month, but I haven't had any quarrels with anyone, John."

"What about your outside business interests? Do you have any enemies that would wish you harm out there? Where's your husband?"

"Ex-husband. Shit, John. Who knows? He ran off with our twenty-two-year-old babysitter two years ago. She wasn't even a babysitter anymore. He stalked her until he could get in her pants after she turned eighteen. The last I heard from him he was in the south of France with the little cunt. I don't speak to him. We talk through our lawyers."

"So, he is fighting for a piece of your family's business?"

"Wouldn't you? I had a pre-nup, but you know how those things go. He's Kristy's stepfather. We married when Kristy was three."

"Do you know where her biological father is?"

"We parted before Kristy was born. It's a long story. Can I get to my daughter, please? We can talk about this later."

"Phil will drive you to the hospital." John stood but sat back down next to Liz on her bed. "I found her alive, Liz. I don't know that she can be saved. Everyone is doing the best that they can, but if I were you, I would hold to the position that Kristy is dead."

"I'm not a defeatist, John, but I am a realist. I am going to the hospital with all hope that my baby can be saved, then we'll deal with it from there."

John helped her to her feet, and Phil held her under her arm as he walked her out of the bedroom and down to his car while asking John to take care of the scene. He said he would have his CSI team on-site within minutes and would keep things out of the media as long as he could.

CHAPTER THREE

*"'What if it doesn't work' isn't
part of your vocabulary."*

Jim coughed hard. "Jesus Christ, John! You have a blood eagle survivor?"

"Yes. Fifteen-year-old Kristy Yates."

"Wait … the daughter of Liz Yates at the Secret Service?"

"Yes, Jim."

"Where is the kid now?"

"In surgery at Northridge Hospital. They have her on a heart lung machine while they try to undo what this monster has done."

"Any motive?"

"None. Liz received a phone call early this morning that her daughter had been taken but was being returned, and she came home to find her on her knees on her bed anchored to the ceiling by her lungs spread out like wings. If I hadn't been paying close attention and realized she was still alive, law enforcement or the coroner would have killed her."

"Fuck, John. Black's dead, and Yate's kid was blood eagled, too. What the fuck is going on?"

"I don't know, but we have one sick killer out there, and I doubt the killer knows that Kristy is still alive. If she survives, she will be the key to this case."

"We can't sit around waiting and hoping that the kid survives and that we can talk to her. We have to get moving."

"Moving where? Where are we going to move? There are no suspects. We have one dead and another fighting for her life. I checked Black out. He was a high functioning autistic man and an avid reader. He spent the last decade reading books at the Los Angeles Public Library. He was well educated with a Ph.D. in philosophy, but he never used the degree. He read. Period. That was the whole of his life. Lester Black's assets are all in a trust for his son. Only the robotics division of the company is operating in the trust. The rest of the businesses were sold off after the father's murder. Black Robotics and AI Inc. is the only entity left operating, and the sales made Black one really, really rich man."

"Who runs the corporation?

"The CEO is a woman named Beverly Hampton."

"Really?"

"Do you know her?"

"Yeah. We saw each other a few times years ago when she was in college."

"She's pretty young, Jim. She just turned thirty-three this year. You were married to Barbara for the past seven, so you were dating a woman in her late teens or early twenties?"

"She was twenty-three. It was a puppy love thing. I was teaching a class at UCLA on criminal justice as a guest lecturer. We had a few cups of coffee and a dinner and ended up in bed."

"I see, and how did it end?"

"Fine. It was a few months after I finished my time at the university. We drifted apart. She was a kid. I was a grown man. It was a fling, John. That's all."

"Well, was there anything unusual about her? Did you teach her any new ways to have sex? Perhaps help her to experiment?"

"What the fuck are you getting at?"

"You know exactly what I'm getting at. You and Barbara and your kinky young life. You two were all over the place in the world of strange sex."

"Erotica, John. We played all types of games, but they were harmless."

"Hardly. I know all of the stories that Barbara and you shared. There isn't anything in the world of bizarre sex that you don't know."

"Fuck you, Swenson. It's been fifteen years. I don't remember everything we did. I took her to some clubs, introduced her to people. We weren't a couple per se. She was a horny young kid with a crush, and I was a dirty old man who liked her a lot. Are you fuckin' suggesting that I might have corrupted her or made her into an evil person?"

"No, Jim … just drilling for the nerve. How do you like it?"

"I fuckin' don't."

"We need to pay Beverly a visit. As long as there is no tension between the two of you, I want you and Sam there as well as Chris."

"There's no fuckin' tension, John. Set the meeting and tell me when and where."

Jim hung up the phone and stormed over to his office window, lighting a cigarette as he went. The side door to his office was open, and Sam could see him and asked, "Are you okay?"

"Yeah. Why?"

"That was a heated conversation. I'm sorry, but it was a little hard not to overhear." Sam was now standing next to him with her own cigarette in her hand, which he lit before snapping his Zippo shut.

"It wasn't as heated as you might think. John was just giving me a taste of my own shit."

Sam nodded and took a long hit off her cigarette and stood staring out the office window. She looked around at the glass and asked, "Has anyone ever washed these windows before?"

"How the fuck would I know?"

"Well, I can hardly see out of them. I know it's an old building, but we should have our windows washed every once in a while, don't you think?"

"No. It's better not having to see the shithole of a city on the other side of the glass."

Kristy Yates was face down on the operating table and was being prepped to be hooked up to a heart lung machine while a team of surgeons and nurses were cooling her body. Doctor Harvey Stein was a cross trained transplant surgeon with decades of experience. He stood looking over Kristy's body as his team worked to cool her down, so her heart and lungs could be stopped for surgery. "Jesus Christ, Sara. I'm a transplant surgeon. I've never performed a procedure like this in my career. How the fuck am I supposed to get this poor kid's heart and lungs back in place?" Jade was up in the viewing suite with Sara as was Jessica.

Jade called down, "Harvey, it's actually very simple. Once the girl is fully on CPB, you stop the heart and respiration, then you gently push each of the lungs back into the chest cavity and then close the spread ribs like a car door one at a time. I've looked at the cuts on the ribs, and they were perfectly cut as if with a laser and will go right back into place. Use both cerclage wire and Kryptonite bone cement, and the ribs will lock in place and heal very, very quickly."

"Kryptonite is still in clinical trials and is not FDA approved, Jade."

Jade looked at Sara and asked, "Is your hospital enrolled in that trial?"

"We just got our first batch. No one has used it yet, but we are permitted in extreme situations. Have you worked with the stuff?"

"Jessica and I have used it in the morgue on cadavers to test the integrity of the glue. Our patients are dead, but I can tell you the shit dries in a matter of minutes and within hours we had to break the bones with hammers or saws. The shit works that well. I know it's been used in Canada for several years with great results. If you have the stuff, use it."

"I don't know, Jade. This is a fifteen-year-old with severe trauma. What if it doesn't work?"

"What if it doesn't work? Sara, that poor girl is going to have to have both her back put back together and then her sternum cracked for open heart surgery to reset her heart and lungs. 'What if it doesn't work' isn't part of your vocabulary here. If Harvey just wires her back shut and then flips her over and even one of those ribs slips, she's dead. You have an opportunity to save this kid's life and help advance science. If she ends up on my autopsy table, Jessica and I will be experimenting on her after our official duties are done."

"How many times have you used this stuff?"

"Dozens, right Jess?"

"Dozens of times, Sara. Like Jade said, we have only used it on the dead, but the stuff seems to really work. You have a humpty dumpty situation down there, and you have to try and put her back together. If she dies, you will put it under review, but you have the clearance, you have the materials; there is absolutely nothing to lose by using the glue and everything to lose if he just wires her shut."

"Jesus Christ. Are you two comfortable assisting Harvey?"

Jade looked hard at Sara, "Sara, we don't have privileges. We're board certified surgeons, but we work on the dead not the living. I want the kid to live, but we're not qualified to perform this type of procedure."

"You don't have to touch the patient. Just consult. I will give you both temporary clearance. I've seen your work. If you help Harvey and his team put, as Jessica just stated, Humpty Dumpty back together again, she has a chance. He doesn't know the glue. You do."

"I will not touch the patient, Sara. Good or bad, that is on Harvey and his people. We are simply in there to consult and nothing more."

"That's all I'm asking. I can have the glue in the operating room by the time you two have scrubbed."

Jade looked at Jessica and asked, "Are you willing to do this?"

"Yes, but if shit goes sideways and I can save that girl, I won't stand by and let her die. I will intervene. I took an oath."

Jade shook her head. "Jess, we're simply consulting on a procedure."

"No. This is about doing something that has never been done that I'm aware of, and I want that girl to have every opportunity to survive. So, just know if things go sideways and I can save her I will do it even if it costs me my license."

Sara was staring down into the theater, "If you and Jade assist with the operation, even if the patient dies, you will not lose your licenses. As the hospital administrator I have the authority to grant you surgical rights, so if Harvey needs hands or you two think of a better way to do it, then talk to Harvey."

"Sara, Harvey is already freaking out down there. He is way out of his element. Jessica and I are used to putting the dead back together every day. It's our job. Now, we have an opportunity to save this kid's life. However, I think it would be wise if you and Karen were in there with us."

"Why? Harvey and his team know what they're doing."

"No, they don't. Jessica and I can manhandle those organs and get them back in place if we need to. We can close her back and then work with the team to flip her for the rest of the operation, but time is of the essence. The longer she's on bypass the greater the chance of long-term brain injury. We have to work fast. With you and Karen in the room, I think it will calm Harvey down, and he will have four extra sets of hands to complement the other two or three." Sara picked up a white phone in the gallery and paged Karen to the operating room. Jade smiled, as did Jessica. "Now, let's go save this little girl's life."

CHAPTER FOUR

"Dear God! Does she know?"

J ohn and Chris were seated in the lobby of Black Robotics along with Sam and Jim. No one was speaking as Chris thumbed through a magazine. Beverly Hampton's assistant entered and invited the four back to Ms. Hampton's office and asked if she could get anyone anything.

Jim was standing near a large window looking down over a conveyor belt of robots. Beverly walked into the room and saw him and exclaimed, "Jim! Jim O'Brian!" She ran over to him and gave him a huge hug and kiss with full passionate tongue action. Jim was taken by surprise but reciprocated as the others looked on. She pulled away from him and then hugged him again. "I thought I would never see you again. Jesus! You look good. Have you been working out?"

"Only if you count lifting a scotch glass to his lips," Sam replied snidely.

Beverly turned to see John standing along with Sam and Chris. "Oh God! I am so sorry, Jim. I was so excited to see you that I didn't realize there were others here. Please forgive me for being so forward. Jim and I are former lovers."

Sam looked Beverly up and down. She had short blond hair, green eyes, and a peaches and cream complexion. She was dressed in a business suit that showed off all of her curves, and Sam's mouth fell open at the sight of her. "I'm sorry. Did you say that you and Jim were lovers?"

"Yes, Sheriff Pritchard. It's such a pleasure to meet you. I have read such good things about you." She looked at John and Chris with more of a frown on her face, "Agents Swenson and Mantel."

"Have we met?" Chris asked.

"Not formally but some of our computer and robotic equipment ended up in the Bureau's hands after being used in crimes, and we never got it back."

Chris shook his head "We've had equipment of yours that was used in crimes?"

"Yes."

John spoke up, "Ms. Hampton's company creates robotics for many industries. Unfortunately, some of that equipment ended up in our hands as evidence in a couple of crimes. Do you recall those crimes, Ms. Hampton?"

"I would rather leave the past in the past."

"I'm sure you would, but the past never stays there, does it?"

"What are you insinuating, Agent Swenson?"

"It's Deputy Director Swenson, Ms. Hampton, and I'm not insinuating anything. I am asking a question. Do you recall the situations that caused us to impound your robotics equipment?"

"Yes. Is that why you're here?"

"No, no, Ms. Hampton. We are here to talk to you about Mr. Steven Black."

"What about Steven?"

"When was the last time you saw him?"

"Yesterday at his home. I was delivering some information. Why?"

"Please have a seat, Ms. Hampton." Beverly sat down behind her desk, and John towered over her desk. "As I know you are aware, Mr. Black has no next of kin."

"I'm aware. I'm also the closest person to him." Beverly paused as she answered with a bit of a quiver in her voice.

"Do you know if anyone has had any type of altercation with Mr. Black? Someone that would wish him harm?"

Beverly began shaking. "No. Steven is loved by everyone." Beverly looked at Jim with pleading eyes and asked, "Jimmy, what's going on?" Jim put his fingers to his lips as John spoke.

"Ms. Hampton, Mr. Black's body was discovered in some bushes behind the Los Angeles Public Library this morning."

"His body?"

"Yes, ma'am."

"Are you telling me that Steven is dead?"

"That's exactly what I'm saying. Mr. Black was the victim of a savage killer."

"Savage? I don't understand. Steven was murdered?"

"Yes, Ms. Hampton. I can't give specifics at this time, but we're notifying you since he had no next of kin."

Beverly began bawling and threw herself into Jim's arms. "This can't be, Jimmy. This can't be."

"I'm afraid it is."

"Who the hell would want to hurt Steven? He was a gentle, loving man. He never did anything to anyone. He was smart and in love."

John's head bolted to the side. "In love?"

"Well, he was in love, but it wasn't reciprocated as far as I know."

"Who was he in love with?"

"The head librarian at the Los Angeles Public Library. Joanne Fontaine. He was just head over heels for her. Had been for years. He tried so hard to court her. I even spoke to her a few times on his behalf. I pleaded with her to just go on one date with Steven, but she refused."

Jim asked, "If Steven was such a nice person, why wouldn't Ms. Fontaine go out with him?"

"She told me she was celibate and that she would not want to lead Steven on. She told me she thought very highly of him but that she had made some life choices that she was committed to and that it would be dishonest to see Steven outside of the library." Beverly paused and then looked at John and asked, "Dear God! Does she know?"

"She found his body; however, it was face down, and she is not aware that the man she found this morning was Mr. Black ... at least not yet. We will tell her before the end of the day."

Jim released Beverly, and she went back to her desk and took out a box of Kleenex and wiped her eyes. "So, you can't tell me how Steven died?"

"Not at this time, Ms. Hampton. We will release more information as it is available." John paused. "When you last saw Mr. Black, did he appear to be in any distress, worried, concerned?"

"Not at all. He was happy, funny. He showed me his most recent read, which was *Ulysses* by James Joyce. He had a fascination with Joyce and was reading *Ulysses* for the third or fourth time. He was a dedicated academic; he just couldn't function well without a set routine."

"Tell me about his routine."

"Steven had obsessive compulsive disorder, which is common in people with Asperger's. So, everything had to be in its place. Anything out of order would send him into fits. He had the same routine for at least a decade. He would wake at six a.m. The servants would have his breakfast set for him at six thirty. He would eat, read the paper, shower, dress, and then leave for the library, always arriving fifteen minutes before it opened. He had one particular seat at the library that he preferred and after some negotiations and donations to the library his favorite table and chair were made his permanent domain about six years ago. Joanne was helpful in getting that accomplished, but as you know money speaks louder than anything else, so the library has broken ground on the Black

Family Wing to open in 2021. I believe Steven dedicated it last year with a silver shovel ceremony. He would read all day, taking breaks for food at one of three restaurants that he liked, and then he came home after the library closed."

"How did he get around?"

"The bus was his favorite means of transportation, but he always had a private car that would drive him twenty-four hours a day."

"Do you know if he used his car yesterday?"

"I have no idea, Director Swenson. It's easy enough to find out. I need just call the house to see if he used it, but I doubt it."

"And how would he finish his day?"

"The same way he started it. Dinner, reading, a shower, then bed by ten."

"And this was his whole life?"

"Yes."

Jim laughed. "Damn boring life if you ask me."

Beverly shot Jim a look. "You don't understand his condition, Jim. Please don't make jokes. Steven was very happy in his life."

John sat down in one of Beverly's chairs and asked, "Would he befriend strangers? Even the high functioning are leery of strangers."

Beverly shook a little. "Well, he did have one other compulsion."

"And what was that?"

"Sex."

"Sex? As in prostitutes?"

"High priced escorts, well vetted and very expensive. He did have a tendency to sometimes stalk around the library after closing time. He would follow Joanne. She lives only a few blocks down. He would also walk the park near the library where there were prostitutes."

"And would he bring them home with him?"

"Not that I ever heard about, but he did have an appetite for street walkers, and he told me stories of some of the things he would do in and around the park."

"Did he ever go with these prostitutes to motels or their homes?"

"Yes. It was the one huge fear I had about him. At home, everything was controlled, but when he would get with one of the street walkers he would sometimes not come home until the wee hours of the morning."

"But you said he had an unchanging routine."

"He did, but sex would easily throw that routine off, and if he didn't come home, I would always get a call from his head of house staff."

"Was there such a call last night?"

"Yes."

John took a deep breath. "You talked us through this charade instead of just telling us he was with a prostitute last night?"

"His reputation is important."

"His reputation means nothing now, Ms. Hampton, as he is dead, and had you told us this from the start we could have people canvasing the area around the library and talking to people. You do know that that is a very, very dangerous part of the city, right?" Beverly nodded. "You do know that there are homeless encampments, drug dealers, as well as prostitution, right?"

"Yes, Mr. Swenson. Steven has been in that area for years. He knew a lot of the locals, and he knew a lot of the hookers."

"Do you know who any of these women were?" John paused. "We are talking about women, right?"

"Of course. Steven wasn't gay. He was straight."

"Do you know what type of sex he was into?"

Beverly recoiled. "What kind of question is that? How and why would I know?"

Jim spoke up, "Beverly, if Mr. Black liked certain types of sex acts it could be important to the case and to finding his killer."

"Jim, I never slept with Steven. I have no idea what his sexual tastes were. It was not a subject that we ever spoke about. Our relationship was more like brother sister. I knew of his needs and that he had sex. For answers on that, you should speak to the woman who ran Steven's house and who most likely has the names and contact information for the women that Steven at least saw at his home."

"And who would that be, Bev?" Jim asked.

"Lisa Sims. She was Steven's head of staff for the mansion. She would have all of that information. When can I see Steven?"

Jim shook his head. "I don't know, Bev. This is a brand new investigation, and his body is with the coroner right now. It will most likely be a week or more."

John asked, "What is the protocol in the trust in the event of Mr. Black's death?"

"I have no idea. That would be up to the accountants and lawyers. I will continue to run daily operations until the trustee decides what to do with the assets of the estate."

"You're working on several government projects, aren't you Ms. Hampton?"

"Yes, Director. We have many projects in the works and several others in the bidding stage."

"I see your organization provided robots to Joling Farms. Is that correct?"

"It is, but that was before I took over operations."

"Your organization has also created robots with artificial intelligence for many, many other businesses, correct?"

"Yes, but I don't understand what that has to do with Steven's death. AI and robotics is an ever-evolving industry, director. We have clients across the country and around the world. We create robotics for the computer industry for assembling motherboards and shrinking components to the auto industry as well as many, many others. The Joling Farms fiasco had nothing to do with our robots."

"They were used to slaughter tens of thousands of people."

"And how is that our fault? We bid and then built robots based on the client's requests. From what I have read, the Blacks had a long-term relationship with Joling. We built the robots but were not and are not responsible for how they were used."

"I understand that, Ms. Hampton, but if a contract came to you to build a robot that looked suspicious, would you report it to the authorities?"

"Suspicious in what way?"

"I don't know. Something that would stand out as not for a legitimate business use."

"Director, I don't see every contract. Those are handled by our sales and engineering departments. I oversee general operations for this corporation. Who am I to judge a project as being good or bad or to know whether robots are going to be used for good or bad purposes? A robot is an inanimate object with no feelings or thoughts of its own. It's the human operating and programming the device that is responsible. But, hypothetically speaking, if we were approached or I was approached by a company or individual to create a robot that I felt was odd, yes, I would report it to the authorities. But in my three years here, I haven't seen anything like that. Now, who do I contact with regard to Steven's body? I need to start making arrangements for him as well as getting this news to the trustee, so that the gears can get moving on dealing with his death."

"Doctor Jade Morgan, the Los Angeles County Coroner, will be in touch when Mr. Black's body can be released. You can begin the process of making funeral arrangements, but, as I stated, it will most likely be a week or more before you can move on them."

"Has this been released to the media yet?"

"We don't release information like this until the next of kin has been notified."

"So, now that I know, should Black Robotics release a statement?"

"I will leave that to you and your public relations people. We aren't providing any information to the media at this time."

Beverly stood and shook John's hand. "I didn't mean to be rude, director. I'm in shock."

"I understand, Ms. Hampton, and we are doing everything in our power to find Mr. Black's killer or killers and to bring them to justice."

John handed her his card, and Jim handed her one of his. He looked into Beverly's red eyes and smiled weakly as he pulled her into his arms and hugged her. "I'm sorry you had to learn about Steven this way."

"Jimmy, is there a good way to learn about these types of things?"

"No, Beverly, there never is."

John called the hospital from his truck and was told that Kristy was in surgery and that Doctor Harvey Stein was being assisted by Doctor Swenson and Doctor Mantel. John asked if Liz Yates was at the hospital and was told that she was there with some family members. He hung up the line, and Jim, Chris, and Sam were all looking at him. "What?" he asked.

Jim got into his face. "Beverly Hampton is a sweet, well educated, young woman, John. I've known her for many years, and the way you treated her in there was an inquisition instead of a notification of a death."

"Everyone is a suspect until they aren't, Jim. That's the code."

"Yeah, well, the code stops with Beverly. You shocked and upset her for no fuckin' reason. All you had to do was tell her that Black was dead. But no, you had to walk her down streets and ask questions that she would have no answers for and bring up cases like Joling that happened when she was in fuckin' middle school. What the fuck were you thinking?"

"I wanted reactions, and I got them. Black Robotics is a multibillion dollar business. Ms. Hampton is paid a lot of money, and she holds a substantial stock interest in the company."

"One, how do you know all of this? And two, what the fuck are you thinking?"

"I did some digging into Ms. Hampton's background. You're right. She is well educated. She got this job right out of college through the trustee who she knows well or should I say has allowed him to do her well."

Jim's face contorted. "Fuck you, John. She didn't sleep her way into this job."

"Yes, she did. Don't get me wrong. She has all of the qualifications, but when she was in grad school, she needed cash, and she ended up in a relationship with the trustee of Black's estate."

"Who the fuck is the trustee of the estate?"

"You aren't going to like it."

"Fuckin' try me!"

"Trevor Craig."

"Trevor Craig? The fuckin' stump monkey lawyer who took over Howard Cohen's law firm?"

"Yep. Howard was the Black's original trustee and was close friends with Lester Black. At the time of Lester Black's death, Trevor Craig was clerking for Howard. When he got out of law school, Howard took him under his wing, and he became more than a rising star. He became a damn comet. He was Howard's secret weapon in many, many cases. Then after Howard's suicide and the killings at the firm had been resolved, he took over as the head of the firm but kept Howard's name front and center in memoriam to him. So, the firm is now known as Cohen, Craig, and Mars. Craig took over all of Howard's clients, Black being one of them. He is also a professor at UCLA's School of Law and holds a chair in the business department at the school. That's where he and Beverly met and started up a relationship."

"How the fuck do you know all of this?"

"It's my job. As soon as I knew who Black was, I started making calls. By the time I got to the corporation and Ms. Hampton, I received a call from an old friend, Justice Robinson, who had heard about Black's death through the grapevine and thought I should know about this relationship. Larry told me that Craig 'took care' of Beverly her last two years of school and that they have a close relationship even now."

"I fuckin' hate lawyers."

"I know. What I don't know is how this trust is administered and what, if anything, Ms. Hampton and Mr. Craig stand to gain from Mr. Black's death. Now you understand why I was needling her?"

"I know she's loose with men, John, but I still don't believe she had anything to do with Black's murder."

"But the rule still applies, doesn't it?"

"Yeah."

Jim lit a cigarette and stormed off to his car. Chris and Sam were standing in stunned silence until Sam asked, "So, what now, John?"

"I want you and Chris to go back to the library and let Ms. Fontaine know that Mr. Black is deceased."

Chris looked over at Jim puffing on his smoke and staring at the sky. "And what about you and Jim?"

"Jim and I need to pay a visit to Trevor Craig to see what he will volunteer about the trust."

"Why not just get a subpoena?"

"No grounds at this moment. We have two people who have been tortured in the same manner: one a billionaire and the other the child of a federal employee. I have jurisdiction in the federal case. Sam has jurisdiction in the Black case. Right now, we have to work this from both sides until we can connect them, then I will have leverage in the matter."

Sam asked, "So, do you want me to give Ms. Fontaine details?"

"She found the body, Sam. She knows the details. I want you to let her know and let me know how she reacts."

Sam called out to Jim, "I'm going downtown with Chris to speak to the librarian."

"Fine!" Jim walked back over to John and asked, "So, who are we going to see?"

"Trevor Craig."

"This is Trevor."

A voice on the other end of the phone said, "Steven Black is dead."

"How and when? I haven't heard anything about this."

"His body was found outside the Los Angeles Public Library."

"Jesus! Does Beverly know?"

"I assume so. The FBI and Sheriff's Department were on scene, and your old pals John Swenson and Jim O'Brian were there, too."

"Why would Swenson be on a local crime scene?"

"Beats the hell out of me, but he was."

"How do you know about Steven's death?"

"I'll explain that to you later. Right now, I have visitors."

CHAPTER FIVE

*"Alright, people. This poor
kid has endured hell."*

Harvey was sweating profusely as one of the nurses wiped his forehead. Jade and Jessica had been able to put the organs back into Kristy's body, and Harvey was pushing each rib back into position over her spinal column.

"Retractor, please, and I need more suction. I can't see a damn thing." Jade was suctioning out the wound as Harvey worked. Once the last rib had been put back in place, he looked at the glue and then Jessica and asked, "You really know how to use this stuff?"

"Yes, Doctor Stein. Jade and I know it well."

"You know how to use it on the dead not the living, Doctor Holmes."

"Is this your first interaction with this bone glue?"

"I have read a lot about it, but I just haven't felt comfortable using it. The speed with which it sets up is alarming to me. I prefer the tried and true."

"We don't have that luxury here, Harvey. Those ribs have to be set before we put this kid on her back to finish the surgery," Jade said calmly.

"Yes, well, I must defer to your expertise, doctors. I am now assisting, and you are taking the lead."

Jade nodded and looked at Sara for approval, which came in the form of a nod.

"Okay, people, listen up. This glue bonds the bone quickly, so we can't screw around. Jessica, you will ensure that each rib is in its proper position. Sara, you will then put in a temporary clip. Next, I will need Karen and Jess to gently pull the bone away from the spine, and I will place the glue. Once I've done that, release the bone and apply pressure for twenty seconds."

Harvey looked on and asked, "Twenty seconds? That's all the time you need to get a bond?"

"Yes, Harvey. Then, we will put the temporary pins in until all of the ribs have been reattached, at which point Sara will move rib by rib and pull the pins. Karen, you and Jessica will then follow Sara down the spine and prepare to close the wound. Once I have the final bone fused, Sara will pull the final pin, and you two will close. After that, everyone will need to help flip her."

Sara called out to the anesthesiologist, "Peter, is the patient's airway clear for the flip?"

"Yes, doctor."

"Doctor Evans, are the CPB machine lines free to move when we flip her?"

"Yes, Doctor Swenson. There will be no lag. I will be able to assist in moving the patient and the tubing."

"How long has the patient been on bypass?"

"Two hours and forty minutes."

"Alright, people. This poor kid has endured hell, but we have to get her fixed and warmed up fast. We can't go longer than five hours."

Harvey nodded as everyone took their positions, and the bone fusion began.

John and Jim arrived at Trevor Craig's office at just after one p.m. They announced themselves and asked to see Mr. Craig. As they sat in the main lobby, Jim said, "Eerie, huh? The last time I was here was when Cohen cut his throat."

"I'm pretty sure that they have cleaned up that mess, Jim."

"The fuck they have. They're still trying to prosecute lawyers, judges, and others in the legal world. Howard took the easy way out. They would have locked that fucker up and thrown away the key."

Jim paused as a pleasant young woman came out. "Director Swenson, Sheriff O'Brian, my name is Danni Bronte, Mr. Craig's assistant. Please follow me." The two men shook her hand and then followed her down the hall to Howard Cohen's former office. She walked them in and said, "Please have a seat. Mr. Craig will be with you shortly. He's just finishing up a court call. Can I offer you anything to drink?" The two men shook their heads, and Danni left the office.

Jim looked around at the updated modern office and its furnishings. "Well, this kid is making bank."

When Trevor entered, he was dressed in a suit and tie with his black hair slicked back like a mobster. His tan skin and white teeth were striking, and his brown eyes were bright and clear. "Good afternoon, gentlemen. I'm sorry to have kept you waiting. How may I be of service?"

"Mr. Craig, we have learned that you are the trustee for the Black estate," John said firmly.

"Indeed, I am. It was one of the first cases I took over after Howard Cohen's passing."

"Mr. Black was found murdered this morning downtown, and we paid a visit to Beverly Hampton as she is the closest thing to next of kin to let her know what has happened."

"I am aware of Mr. Black's passing."

"Who made you aware of that?"

"I received a call from a reporter asking me for a comment, and I had none as at that moment I was unaware of his death. I then called Beverly, who told me that you two gentlemen had been to see her and that Steven was dead."

Jim was seated straight up in an office chair as John continued. "Do you know of anyone who would have wished Mr. Black harm?"

"No, not at all. He was a very nice man, well respected, too. He had his disabilities, but he braved them well, and I am in shock right now at his passing."

"Murder, Mr. Craig. Steven Black was brutally murdered last night or early this morning."

"Why would anyone want to hurt Steven?"

"That was a question we hoped you could answer."

"Please, Director Swenson, call me Trevor. I know that you and my former boss had your ups and downs through the years, but he did speak highly of you." Trevor looked at Jim who had a light smile on his face.

"And when he spoke of me?"

"I think we both know how you and Howard felt about each other, Sheriff O'Brian. Your feelings toward those of us in the legal profession are legendary."

"Jesus! Did you hear that, John? I'm a legend in the legal world. What a fuckin' joke."

John asked, "Trevor, do you know of anyone who would want to hurt Mr. Black?"

"No sir. Mr. Black was a well-loved member of this community."

"What is going to happen to the trust?"

"I can't answer that question right now. I just learned of his passing. I'm sorry, murder, and I have to pull the trust paperwork to see how the trust is to be handled."

"I understand that Mr. Black has a half-sister?" John asked.

"Yes. His father had a child from his first marriage, but she has no claim to the estate. She was written out of the will and trust while Lester Black was living."

"Why did he have such animosity toward his daughter?"

"I have no idea, Mr. Swenson. She's much older than Steven, and to be honest, I have never met the woman."

"Why would you?"

"I wouldn't. I know that Howard had contact with her after her father died, but I have no idea what type of relationship he had with her. There are no notes of conversations, and there has never been any action taken by the sister or her mother against the trust."

"Do you know her name?"

"Bailey Ellen Black. I think she goes by Ellen or Ell, but I'm not sure." John was typing on his tablet as Trevor spoke. "May I ask what you are typing?"

"I'm looking for information on Ms. Black."

"I would think you would need more than a name, Director Swenson. There are a lot of people with that name in LA."

"Not connected to Lester Black."

John kept typing, and Jim asked, "How well do you know Beverly Hampton?"

"I don't think that is any of your business, Sheriff."

"I think it is. I have known her for many years."

"Yes, I am aware. I heard through the grapevine about your tryst when she was in school. That was not exactly ethical."

"You really want to get into ethics, Mr. Craig? I have it on good authority that you were her sugar daddy for the last two years of her Ph.D. studies at UCLA. I understand that you stepped down as the chair of that department to have that relationship."

John was still typing, and Trevor was clearly nervous. "Ms. Hampton and I had a consensual sexual relationship while she was in school. I take issue with you calling me her 'sugar daddy.'"

"Take issue with it all you like. It's a fact. After that, she graduated and landed a position as the head of Black Robotics and AI where you were the trustee over the estate. I think that there is some room for investigation of this relationship and now her position of power over a large corporation."

John interrupted, "Interesting."

"What did you find?"

"Well, Jim, it appears that Ms. Black is an employee of the U.S. Postal Service here in Los Angeles. She's a letter carrier and has been for nearly twenty years. I didn't find any offenses in her record, and she appears to live a relatively humble life."

Trevor looked on. "As I stated, I don't know Ms. Black. She has nothing to do with the estate or trust. I do know, however, that Lester Black left specific instructions that she was not to be notified upon his death or told anything about the trust and estate."

"Are you telling us that Ms. Black is not aware that her father is dead?"

"Again, I know what Howard told me about the father's wishes. I have not pulled the trust records as I have just learned of Mr. Black's death, so there is little I can add. She may or may not know her father's dead. I imagine the police have not released the information on Steven's death to the media yet, correct?"

"The case belongs to the Sheriff's Department, but I have asked them to keep it under wraps as we work together on it."

"Why would the FBI get involved in this matter?"

"Because Black Robotics and AI is working on several high-level government contracts."

"But Steven had nothing to do with the company or the contracts."

"Mr. Craig, if I took the word of everyone who claimed they knew nothing about something, there would never be an arrest made in a case. Everyone is a suspect until they are not. Now, when you pull the trust records on Black's estate, would you be so kind as to notify my office, so we can have a look at them?"

"Not without a subpoena, Director Swenson."

John pulled out his cellphone and hit speed dial and spoke to the person on the other end of the line, "This is Deputy Director John

Swenson. Please request a subpoena for the financial and trust records of The Black Family Holdings Living Trust; Black Robotics and AI Incorporated; Black Holdings LLC; and the personal financial records of Mr. Steven Black."

There was a pause, and Trevor stood up as John and Jim were already standing.

"Please leave my office this minute."

John ignored Trevor and continued his conversation. "Homicide and protection of records. I need it served on the trustee of the estate, Attorney Trevor Craig at the offices of Cohen, Craig, and Mars."

"You can't just do whatever the hell you like. There is due process, Director."

John continued with his phone call. "Okay, thank you, and put the U.S. Attorney's Office on notice that Mr. Craig will file a TRO to stop the enforcement of the subpoena, so be prepared to appeal it to the ninth circuit. I will call Chief Justice Robinson to let him know where we are."

John hung up the line, and Trevor was furious. "Get the hell out of my offices this instant."

"My men will be here in a half hour, Mr. Craig. Don't do anything stupid."

John walked out with Jim behind him, laughing. "You just asked an attorney not to do anything stupid? Jesus Christ, John! That's like asking water not to be wet."

Joann saw Sam and Chris enter the library and began to shake violently as they approached the front counter. Sam was in uniform, and Chris showed his ID. Joann stood up with weak knees, and Chris and Sam stepped behind the counter in time for Chris to catch her. He helped her to her office, and after sitting her down, she looked at the two of them and said, "The dead man I found this morning was Steven Black, wasn't it?"

"Yes, Ms. Fontaine. We have had some interesting conversations over the past several hours about you and Mr. Black," Sam said softly, and Chris stood near Joann, so she wouldn't fall out of her chair.

"What type of conversations?"

"Conversations that validate your story about your relationship with him."

"I had no relationship with Mr. Black. I thought I made that clear. My God! That was his body brutalized in the bushes by the side entrance?"

"Yes, Ms. Fontaine. We simply came here to inform you that it was him."

"Thank you. I mean, I don't know what to say. I just talked to him last night and now he's dead."

Sam drew a deep breath. "That's how life turns. We deal with this every day. It's important to let the people you love and care about know how you feel because you never know when your number will be called."

"That was balls to the wall, John. You know that tight ass is rounding up every lawyer in the building right now."

"That's what I wanted. I wanted to see the reaction, and it was what I expected."

"So, do you think that Craig is involved?"

"Oh yes, and that living trust is going to unmask others who are in on this killing."

"What about the Yates kid? What the fuck did she do to deserve this?"

"I don't know, Jim, but they are connected. The key is to find out who all of the players are and then try and piece this puzzle together before more are tortured to death."

Jim sat silent for a few seconds then lit a cigarette and hung his arm out the window. "The Iron Eagle just got a lesson in a new form of torture, didn't he?" John nodded. "So, you want the person or persons to meet the same fate at the Eagle's hands?"

"I have known about the blood eagle technique for years. I just never implemented it."

"Why the fuck not?"

"It's just pure torture, Jim. It isn't a way of getting information. In all but a few of my cases I have needed to get information, and it's a little hard to talk when your lungs have been pulled through your back."

"Well, I'm excited to see how this case evolves and to see if the Eagle gets to do a blood eagle killing."

John frowned. "Let's take this one step at a time. Whoever did this had an axe to grind and won't hesitate to kill any one of us to protect their identity."

"Well, considering the amount of time that has passed since the last killing, I have to agree with you. Whoever is doing this is very, very patient and will fall off the radar as fast as they came back on it once they get what they want."

"It's the 'what they want' part of it I'm hoping the trust will expose. Jade told me that the cuts to Yates' ribs were really clean, which tells me that it was most likely done on some type of machine using laser technology."

"Have you talked to Sara?"

"They are in surgery trying to save the kid's life."

"Is Liz at the hospital?"

"Yes."

"What about Bailey Black? Who's going to pay her a visit?"

John pulled his truck off the 110 Freeway and headed into downtown LA. "You and I are."

"She's a fuckin' street jock, John, not an office worker."

"Well, she comes off shift between two and three, and we are at the two thirty hour, so let's just drop by the main post office and see if we can't surprise her."

CHAPTER SIX

"Don't your students
call us doctors of death?"

"The FBI and Sheriff are going after the trust records."

"That was to be expected, but they won't learn anything of substance from them."

"You don't think that they are going to find your secret stake in the business?"

"Not at all."

"How the hell can you be so sure?"

"I have been deeply insulated in the workings of the company. I admit I love the equipment that I have been able to get for my personal use, and I have used it for my passion for the first time in over a decade."

"Does Beverly know?"

"That I have equipment from Black? Yes. She also knows about my stake in the company, but she has no idea who I am. I'm a ghost. Just a killer working in the night."

"I think you overplayed your hand in Steven's murder."

"Hardly. He was a babbling idiot if you ask me, him and his puppy dog crushes, hookers, and call girls. He had his own dark side, and death was the best thing for him."

"How the hell did you get him?"

"I had him seduced by the library. Getting him was the easy part. He had been wandering around down there for over an hour after the library closed. He was a creepy stalker in a lot of ways. She was dressed in a trench coat in a back alley, and as soon as she could lure him back there, she took off the coat showing off her nude body. She told me he came unglued. He was a sucker for a blonde with a hot body. The rest was just getting him into her car. Once I had him, all was fine."

"Did you use a hooker?"

"I have one hooker I use a lot for victims, but I didn't use her for this. She was on the street last night, though, and she knew Steven and the person who assisted, so I got her."

"So, where is she now?"

"Hanging with several of my other angels."

"Why did you release Kristy Yates?"

"I got what I wanted from her. Her mother will learn a valuable lesson about crossing me again."

"I don't get it. The kid was fifteen and had nothing to do with your falling out with Liz. Why torture her like that?"

"First, the best way to hurt your enemy is not by hurting them but by going after the ones they love. Liz loved her daughter deeply, so killing her put her through more agony than if I had done it to Liz herself."

"So, you're going to let Yates live?"

"For a while to let her get the full impact of burying her kid and feeling the deep suffering that comes from the loss. Then, when the moment is right, I will grab her and take her out."

"What about the FBI and Sheriff?"

"It is all part of the process. I'm hardly concerned about them."

"Director Swenson and Jim O'Brian are tough investigators."

"So? I'm a ghost. They will never find me. Well, they will see me and talk to me, but they'll never suspect in a million years that I am the person behind these killings. You, on the other hand, worry me."

"Why?"

"You know who I am. You know the motives behind the killings. I want to trust you, but I am concerned that if the wrong person leans on you, you will crack and that will get the two of us killed."

"I have known your secret for the entire time you have been killing. Why would I throw you under the bus now?"

"I want to believe that you wouldn't. We should have dinner."

"Okay. When and where?"

"I don't know. We haven't seen each other in months. How about that little Mediterranean restaurant in Studio City?"

"The one at City Walk at Universal?"

"No, the little family one on the corner of Riverside Drive and Rose Street."

"Sounds good. What time?"

"Let's meet at seven. I have two angels that I need to take out of the cooler at my house when I get home from work."

"What are you going to do with the bodies?"

"What I have been doing with them for decades — make sure they are dead then grind them into pulp and burn them up in my incinerator."

"Jesus!"

"Oh, relax. I don't plan on making any more kills right now. With Steven out of the way, and Liz reeling from Kristy's death, I plan on freeing my shares in Black, selling them, and then going back to my hobby. No more public displays of my angels, just a nice healthy dose of cash, so I can build my dream home and play area in Bel Air and then live a nice quiet life with my friend. I know he is ready to be exposed to my collection and hobby … taking those that I think best fit my eye as angels and freeing their inner spirits for my pleasure, so I don't have to be bogged down with the distractions of making money to live."

"I will see you tonight."

"Looking forward to it."

"So how did it go with Ms. Fontaine?" John asked Chris over the phone.

"She was pretty shook up. Sam and I left her about a half hour ago. We asked her to keep this to herself while we investigate it, and she agreed. How did it go with Trevor Craig?"

"The subpoena should have been served by now, and the court battle has most likely begun. I called Larry and asked for a favor. If the court goes against us, the U.S. Attorney will appeal to the ninth circuit, and Larry will take care of it. I figure we will have the trust records by tomorrow. Where are you now?"

"Sam dropped me off at the office. I'll be going over case files until you get back."

"Okay, well, Jim and I have one more visit and that is to the half-sister of Steven Black."

"Steven Black has a half-sister?"

"She works for the postal service downtown. We're waiting for her to check in. As soon as we speak to her, I will be back at the office. Has there been any word from Sara or Karen?"

"No. I hope that the kid makes it. I know you think that you are going to be able to see who you're looking for in those documents, but I'm not so sure."

"What do you mean?"

"Think about it, John. Nearly two decades between killings. Two back to back killings or one killing and one near killing so far. I think you are underestimating this killer and his motives."

"What are the main motives for murder, Chris?"

"Money, revenge, God, government, and then just sick pleasure by causing others to suffer."

"I think this killer is in it for both money and suffering."

"Do you have your eye on anyone in particular?"

"Right now, the field is open. I do, however, think that Mr. Craig knows more about the murders than he has said. I also think that Ms. Hampton does as well."

"Why do you want to talk with the half-sister?"

"Just a formality. I have to cover all loose ends." Jim waved at John. "I have to go. Jim is waving me down. Ms. Black must be here. I will see you back at the office as soon as I'm finished speaking with her."

"Okay, on three."

The surgical team lifted Kristy's small body and gently turned her onto her back. All stood watching her vitals as her blood pressure and respiration held firm. Harvey had been at the head of the table while the team worked, and once Kristy was on her back, he looked at Jade and Jessica and said, "I would kill to have you two on my transplant team. That is the most incredible surgical skill and team work it has been my privilege to witness. When this is over, I would like to invite you both to speak at several of my classes."

Jessica laughed. "Don't your students call us doctors of death?"

"Maybe, but when they read the paper I'm going to write and see the film of this surgery, my students, interns, and residents will see you and your skills in a whole new light."

"We're not out of the woods here, folks. Let's crack her sternum and get her heart and lungs in place and operating on their own," Sara said.

Harvey called out, "My patient. Sara, open the sternum. Jade, be ready with the bone saw. Jessica, you're on the rib spreader." There was no hesitation. Everyone did as directed, and in a matter of five minutes Kristy's chest was wide open, her heart and lungs offset but viable. "Jade, if you had this girl on an autopsy table what would you see?"

"Blunt force trauma to the thorax, severe lung bruising, and the offset of the heart would make me believe the kid had been in a car accident or struck by an object, such as a bat. The pericardium and the pericardial fluid are intact, and the heart appears unharmed. Jessica, we need to move the heart back into position. The lungs are partially inflated, so we don't have a collapse."

"I was wondering why you didn't collapse them when you were putting them back into her chest," Harvey said.

"The risk was too great. If they collapsed together, we would likely have never gotten them to function. They have air in them and while it will hurt her when she breathes for the first few days, the risks of pulmonary failure drop exponentially. You're up, Harvey. We have everything set. Run the lines."

Harvey stepped over and looked at the heart and lungs through a high-powered microscope and then pulled it away and ran his hands along the lungs and the heart, checking the aorta and the chambers. "I think we can start to warm her."

The nursing staff began to remove the cooling liquids and bags that they had used to put Kristy into a state of hypothermia to protect her heart, lungs, and other organs. Harvey injected several medications that brought her temperature up gradually. As she warmed, he ordered that blood flow be slowly restored to the heart and lungs.

"Have the crash cart ready. I will need internal paddles if we don't get a natural restart." Sara was standing by as the blood was slowly introduced into Kristy's body.

"Where are we at?" Harvey asked.

"Fifty percent flow."

"Bring her up more." Harvey waited a few more minutes and asked for an update. "Where are we now?"

"Ninety percent, doctor."

"Okay, let's fill her up. It's show time." Everyone in the operating room stared at the flatline on the heart monitor as the cannulas were removed and the incisions closed. Harvey looked up at the clock on the wall. "Ten seconds."

Sara was standing over Kristy's head and whispered, "Come on, Kristy. You can do it."

The respirator was pumping in air, and Kristy's heart was still then started to quiver in her chest. Harvey smiled. "V tach! Paddles."

Sara watched as the clock hit thirty seconds, but Harvey did nothing. The heart began to move with more violent motion, and at the end of a minute it was throwing off beats that were irregular but improving. Harvey handed the paddles back to the nurse as Kristy's heart began to beat stronger and stronger until she had a perfect rhythm.

"Okay, people. Let's close her up."

Sara spoke up, "Harvey, given the shock that her organs have taken, I think we need to reduce the ventilator to see if she will breathe on her own while she is still open."

"What good will that do, Sara? She will breathe, or she won't. We will need to keep her on a ventilator for a day or so, then we will know."

"If there is a lung issue not a brain issue, let's find out now while we have her opened up. If there is an internal issue, we can address it now and not have to put her through a ton of testing or open her up again."

"And if she doesn't respond and it's not lung related?"

Jade spoke up, "Her EEG is normal, Harvey. There is deep brain function. If there are respiratory problems, it will be injury related. I agree with Sara. Let's bring her out enough to allow the autonomic systems to take over."

"It's your hospital, Sara, and this certainly is an unusual case, so let's do it."

Sara order Kristy to be brought out of anesthesia. "Keep her sedated. Just take her to the brink where her autonomic systems will kick in for breathing." The doctor began to bring Kristy out and as he did, she jerked a bit and then struggled against the ventilator. Sara smiled as Kristy was put back under. "She's breathing on her own. She's going to make it. Let's close her up."

Bailey Black was seated in a break room at the main post office when she was paged to come to the front of the building. She put her food down and walked out to where John and Jim were waiting for her. No one made introductions. The man who paged her walked off, and Bailey looked at the two men and asked, "What do you want?" John flashed his ID as did Jim.

"Is there somewhere we can speak privately?" John asked.

Bailey called out to the postmaster, "Harold, I need a private office for a few minutes. Do you have one open?"

"Use the storage office. Are you off-shift?"

"Yeah. I'm just finishing lunch, then I'm out of here."

"Come on, Bailey. We're short-handed today. Work some overtime."

"No can do. I have things to do this afternoon. I will be happy to put in more tomorrow." She looked at John and Jim then John again, "You're one big son of a bitch. Follow me."

The group made it to the back of the building where Bailey invited them in then took a seat and asked, "So, what do you want?"

"Ms. Black, I'm Deputy Director Swenson, and this is Undersheriff Jim O'Brian."

"I can read. I saw your IDs, now what do you want?" Bailey was short and heavy set with long brown hair and hazel eyes. She was pale and a bit gaunt in her face, and her uniform was unkempt.

"We're here about your half-brother, Steven Black."

"What about him? I hope you're not here for a reunion. That won't be happening."

"We've been told you have a great deal of hostility toward your brother."

"Half-brother, and I don't like him. He's a retard, and my old man cut me off decades ago."

Jim spoke up. "Mr. Black was found murdered this morning in downtown LA."

Bailey laughed. "It took them long enough."

"It took who long enough?" John asked.

"Too complicated to get into and not my business."

"Ms. Black, it is our business. Are you saying that you were aware that your brother would be murdered?"

"You two don't know a damn thing about the Black family, do you?"

"Well, I have a feeling we are about to learn something we didn't know."

"My brother was a pedophile." John and Jim looked at each other. "That's right. That hardy man named Steven Black was a sick, twisted pedophile who got his kicks with young boys and girls."

"And how do you know this?"

"Because he fucked two of my coworker's kids fifteen years ago, and my old man was able to buy off the parents, so it would never be reported."

"Then how do you know about it?"

"They came to me and told me about it. I confronted Steven and my father. The two basically kicked my ass, then they kicked me out of the family."

John was sitting close to Bailey, "Where are those coworkers today?"

"I have no idea. One left the post office after the settlement. I understand it was very generous. The other moved out of state shortly after, and, I think, left the postal service as well."

"We would like to find them and speak to them," John said.

"Good luck with that. I don't remember much about them, and there are no police reports that I know of. My father was very good at making people disappear."

"As in killing them?"

"Who knows? Perhaps. My father was not a man you wanted to get on the wrong side of. I don't know if he was a killer or had killers who worked for him. He just made problems go away. He had money, and the person with the money controls the world. My father left my mother and me when I was just ten and married some skank he had been running around with. They had Steven, who was diagnosed with autism, and my father lost it."

"In what way?" John asked.

"I was always a disappointment to him. He wanted a son, and then when he got one, he ended up with a kid that was a retard."

"People who know Mr. Black say he was a kind man and an intelligent one."

"Yeah, well, they didn't know his dark side. He was very, very smart, but my father was unable to use him in business. The skank took off after my father's death and was found dead in Phoenix a few months later of an overdose. There were rumors that Steven had raped his mother after his father's death, and that she couldn't deal with him and his lifestyle. Soon after his mother's death, he found me."

"So, you spent time with him?"

"Yes. He hunted me out when he was twenty. I was thirty-five and living with a roommate in LA. I wasn't keen on seeing him again. It had been at least five or six years. He begged me to forgive him and said that I was all he had in the world and wanted to reconcile."

"So, what happened?"

"I let him into my life."

"And?"

"And it was the biggest mistake I've ever made."

"How so?"

Bailey rolled her eyes. "Do I really have to spell it out for you after all I have told you about that monster?"

Jim had been quiet but leaned forward and said, "He raped you?"

Bailey nodded as tears welled up in her eyes. "I wouldn't call it rape. The first time we had sex he got me drunk and drugged me."

"That's rape, Ms. Black."

"I was furious and wanted him out of my life, but he kept coming back. We started up a very strange relationship that lasted nearly five years."

John was taking notes on his tablet and asked, "How was it strange?"

"After the first time we had sex, I asked him about his mother and the rumors about the two of them. He denied them but told me that he was attracted to me and was sorry for what he did, but he wanted to continue a sexual relationship with me. It just started but over several years began to spin out of control. He started taking me to clubs and bath houses. He had places he would take me where everyone knew him, and there would be orgies and every type of sex you can imagine."

Jim nodded, "So, he liked the underground sex life?"

"Yes. He talked me into having sex with men and women while he watched and vice versa. He talked several of my friends into group sex with us."

"Was there violence?" Jim asked.

"Yes. That's where I drew the line. He started taking me to bondage clubs, and he had me collared as his sub and ordered me to do the most disgusting things. Human toilet, S&M, cutting, whipping, nailing my breasts to boards. All types of things that just were out of control."

"How did you get out?" John asked.

"I ended it. I told him I was out. That someone was going to get hurt or killed, and it wasn't going to be me."

"How did he react?"

"He just threw his hands up and said fine. He told me that he had his eye on a librarian downtown and that he wanted to cool it with the lifestyle he had been living. He had some twisted fantasy that he was going to court her and get her to marry him and have a family. He did a one-eighty before my eyes or so I thought."

"He was still in the underworld of sex?"

"Yes. I would hear stories about him at the clubs and the things he was into. He was getting in with a more and more violent group of people. I was told that the librarian told him she had no interest in him, but he continued to pursue her."

John asked, "And that's it?"

"Pretty much. The last time I spoke to Steven was about a week ago. He told me that he had met a new sex worker who was coming to his house and asked if I had any interest. I hung up on him and that's the last time we spoke."

John put his tablet down and asked, "Do you know the locations of these clubs?"

"A few. As we got into more dark stuff, I was usually blindfolded and carried into the clubs tied and nude. The other clubs were just swingers' places and strip clubs, mostly on the Sunset Strip. Really common places. Augustine's, Leopold's, several Rhino clubs. They are all on the strip. Too many to count. You can walk into any of them and see what they are up to. If you go private in a lot of them, you can get sex, drugs, weapons. Most of the clubs are run by local gangs as fronts. You also have other criminal enterprises that run these types of places, but I don't have to tell you two. This is what you do for a living."

John sat back as Jim stood up and stretched his legs, "I know all of those clubs, Ms. Black, and I know most of the element that runs them and owns them," Jim said.

"Is there any one person that you recall meeting in those years that you felt would hurt your brother?" John asked.

Bailey had a thoughtful look on her face. "There was one gal, a dominatrix, that my brother had a real thing for. She was a latex goddess and was always masked and in tall heels. She let plenty of skin show but never her face."

"Did she have any markings or tattoos?"

"Yeah. She had a tattoo of what she called a blood eagle on her back. It was really, really creepy. I didn't like hanging out in her dungeon."

"A blood eagle tattoo?" John asked.

"Yeah. I talked to her a few times. She was really into Vikings and Norse mythology. She was also into black magic and a lot of other weird shit."

"Did your brother spend a lot of time with her?"

"Oh, yeah. I know that he paid her a ton of money over the years to be his bottom, and she was at his house a lot, too. He told me stories about her. He was fascinated with her because she would never allow him to see her face."

"But he was close to her?"

"As close as a pay-for-sex and bondage worker can be to her john. She didn't work the club scene too much. She had her own dungeon. I think it was at her home. Again, by the time Steven had graduated to her I was his slave, and I was kept blindfolded and nude, especially when going to her dungeon, so I couldn't begin to tell you where it was, who she was, or anything else. You could talk to his house staff, but I'm pretty sure that no one ever saw her face. She was legendary for that."

Jim asked, "Did she go by a trade name?"

"The Eagle's Mistress."

"The Eagle's Mistress?" John asked

"She was totally and completely obsessed with the Iron Eagle serial killer here in LA. I do remember one night at her bar. Steven had allowed me off the collar, and we were sitting at the bar as she poured us drinks. She was telling stories of the Iron Eagle and how in love with him she was. She pulled a scrapbook out from behind the bar and showed it to several of us. It had newspaper clippings as well as all kinds of crime scene photos and police and FBI information in it. She told us that she was desperately looking for him, that they were soulmates, and that once she found him her life would be complete." Jim had his arms folded as he stared at Bailey. John sat silent looking at his tablet and reading over his notes. "Is there anything else, gentlemen? I've had a long day, and I just want to go home and sit in my hot tub and relax."

John and Jim handed her their cards and asked her to call if she remembered anything else about this mistress and her brother's lovers. The two men left the post office, and Jim lit a cigarette as he climbed into the truck. There was silence between the men as John drove in the direction of Jim's office. Jim had taken several deep hits off his cigarette before saying, "We have a real mess here, John."

"Yeah."

"Well, there is a bit of good news."

"Really? And what's that?"

"Well, if we find the bitch with the blood eagle tattoo on her back, we have found our killer."

"So, you think that this person killed Black and attempted to kill Yates?"

"Fuck yeah. Don't you?"

"Just because people engage in bizarre fantasies doesn't mean they're killers, Jim."

"Excuse me, Deputy Director, but everyone is a suspect until cleared. This chick sounds like she is out of her fuckin' mind. She is in love with the Eagle and has followed his every move, according to Ms. Black. I'm sorry, man, but that woman is our killer. She might have had an axe to grind with Black and Yates, but based on the shit that I just heard, the bitch is trying to mimic the Eagle's killings and is in search of him. She also thinks that you two are soulmates, which makes her even more dangerous. You know why?"

"Yes."

"Good. Because if she gets close, if she is successful in drawing the Eagle out and you don't grab her, or if she finds out the Eagle is married to his soulmate, this bitch is going to kill Sara, and I don't think it will stop there, pal."

CHAPTER SEVEN

"That is one fucked up family."

"I can't believe my baby is alive!" Liz Yates was sitting next to Kristy's bed in the cardiac ICU holding her hand and looking up at Sara and Karen with tears running down her face.

"It's going to be touch and go for at least tonight. Her heart is irritated because of the trauma, so we need to monitor her heart rate and blood pressure. I have her in a drug-induced coma and will most likely keep her like that for a day or two."

"Sara, do whatever you need to do to take care of my baby. I'm just amazed that I'm sitting here looking at her beautiful face."

"Kristy still has a long way to go, Liz. Her breasts were shaved off as was most of her abdomen, pubic area, and thigh. The killer didn't mutilate her face like the other victim, but Kristy is going to need reconstructive surgery over the course of months and years. She is going to be in shock over her body's situation. However, the one thing she has going for her is her age. She should heal quickly, and we have already applied new synthetic skin to a lot of wounded areas, which will allow Kristy to grow new skin faster and allow us to work on reconstruction faster as well."

"We will face those challenges over time. Right now, I am sitting here with my baby, and she's alive."

Karen smiled. "If there is anything you need, just call me. I'm on call twenty-four seven for you." Karen handed Liz a card and left the room.

"Liz, I'm sure you have been asked this already, but do you have any idea who would want to do something so cruel to your daughter?"

"Sara, there's no one. Kristy has no enemies that I know of. Someone grabbed her out of her bed, did the horrific things they did, then put her back, thinking she was dead."

"Yes. The key word is they 'think' she's dead!"

John was typing up a report on the interview with Bailey when Chris poked his head into his office and asked, "How did it go with Ms. Black?"

"In a word? WOW!"

"All right. You have my attention." Chris read over the report that John had been putting together, and John watched his face contort as he read. Chris's eyes would grow huge then his mouth would hang open. John chuckled at his reactions as he read the report. When he was finished, he handed the tablet back to John and said, "That is one fucked up family."

"In a word."

"So, there is a dominatrix out there who has a blood eagle tattooed on her back, has the hots for the Eagle, and wants to be his soulmate?"

"It would appear so."

"Did you get any dimensions from Black on the size of the tattoo?"

"It appears to cover her whole back."

"And the chick has a private dungeon in her home somewhere?"

"Yes."

"And Bailey Black has been there but doesn't know where it is."

"That's her story."

"Well, the good thing is we know who our killer is. The hard part is going to be flushing her out."

"I don't know that she's the killer. And even if she is, she's not alone in this. Someone else knows her identity and has been covering for her." John's office phone rang. He looked at his watch and answered.

"Hi honey! How are you doing?"

"Sara, I'm so glad to hear your voice. How is Kristy Yates?"

"Alive, John. It took Harvey Stein and his team as well as Jade, Jessica, me, and Karen, but we were able to put her back together. She is in cardiac ICU in a drug-induced coma, but I'm hoping that I can remove the ventilator tomorrow and bring her out."

"How is Liz?"

"She's doing well. She's with Kristy now. I have to tell you that was the most intense operation I have ever been a part of. This will be a case study when it is all over. How was your day? Any luck figuring out who did this?"

"I have leads. Right now, we're working them. It's been a very strange day for us as well."

"So, what do you know?"

"Right now, very little. I learned that there's a dominatrix out there who's fixated on the Iron Eagle and has a blood eagle tattooed on her back. Oh, and she believes that she and he are soulmates."

"Really?"

"Yeah. She keeps a scrapbook of all of the Eagle's killings and wants desperately to meet him. She's convinced that when they meet, he will fall in love with her."

"Uh huh. Interesting."

"It gets stranger, but I will talk more about that when we get home. It's five thirty. What time do you think you will get out of there?"

"In a few more hours. I want to keep an eye on Kristy. I have called the house, and chef will have dinner for us at ten. Have you released anything on Kristy's murder?"

"No. We have it under wraps. If the killer learns that she survived, he or she might come for her."

"You better put protection on Kristy and Liz because the killer is going to get concerned if they don't see something about her death in the media by tomorrow."

"I agree. I will send a detail out there to secure her. We will need to release something. Chris and I will talk it over with Jim and Sam. I'll let you know when we see each other."

"Okay. I love you, John."

"I love you, too, Sara. I will see you tonight."

Chris had his feet up on John's desk. "You know you have the bait to catch a killer, right?"

"I know, but I don't want to release information on Yates until I have to."

"Well, the killer is watching, John, and if there is no news, things could spin even more out of control."

"Was the subpoena served?" Chris said it was. "Did we win the appeal?"

"Yes."

"So, we should have it by morning?" Chris nodded. "All right. We hold everything close to our chests overnight, and we will go over the documents in the morning."

"We haven't been here together to eat in years." Trevor nodded at Joann sitting across the table from him. "So, how are things with Howard's old firm? Are you settling in?"

"It's been an adjustment. I took over most of Howard's big clients, and I have been in the middle of a battle with the FBI and Sheriff's Department over one of the client's estates."

"You have always been so good at handling conflict."

"That is what I was trained to do, but it doesn't mean that I always enjoy it."

"I thought lawyers always liked conflict."

Trevor laughed as the waiter came over and took his order. Joann sipped a glass of wine and ordered an appetizer. "I understand that you discovered the body of Steven Black this morning?"

"It was horrible. I didn't know it was him at the time. I was told late this afternoon by Special Agent Chris Mantel and Sheriff Sam Pritchard."

"Well, the issue I'm dealing with has to do with Steven Black and the Black estate."

"Why would they be looking into the Black estate?"

"It is a question that I have no answers to. I have only gone over the paperwork quickly before coming out to dinner. Everything appears in order except for one small problem."

"And what's that?"

"Steven gifted himself ten percent of his company several years ago."

"Why is that a problem?"

"He never sold the shares, and from the paper trail it appears that he then gifted those shares to someone else, but they didn't sell the shares either."

"So, what's ten percent of the company worth?"

"As of today? Fifty million dollars."

"Wow! That's some payday."

"Indeed."

The waiter brought the food, and Trevor started eating when Beverly walked up to the secluded table in the back of the restaurant. Trevor said, "I don't believe I need to make introductions here, do I?" Beverly shook her head as did Joann.

"Good evening, Joann. How is the library business?"

"Going well. How is the robotics and AI business?"

"It's been better. With Steven's murder today, things have gotten a bit more convoluted."

"That's why you have Trevor, right?"

"Indeed."

Trevor wiped his mouth and stood. "I'm sorry to dine and dash, but I have to go over the Black trust documents more tonight, so I can try and find out what the FBI wants with them."

"The FBI is in this case?" Beverly asked.

"Unofficially. Right now, it's the Sheriff's Department and LAPD's case, but I learned through the grapevine late this afternoon that Liz Yates' daughter was murdered this morning as well."

Beverly had a shocked look on her face. "Liz Yates with the Secret Service?"

"Yes. Her fifteen-year-old daughter was found brutally murdered. I have no details on the death."

"I haven't heard anything on the news about this."

"I'm sure it will be reported tonight or tomorrow. But that killing is what most likely is going to bring the FBI into this case as Liz is a federal government employee, and it was her daughter. I will know more soon, so if you two will excuse me."

Trevor left, and Joann sipped her wine as the waiter took the two women's orders and left.

"Well, you're quiet, Beverly."

"Why Joann? Why?"

"Steven had become a problem."

"Explain."

"As you know, he has had a fixation on me for years."

"And rightly so. You jumped into the middle of his life when his father was trying to groom him for business. You caught him on the rebound after the fiasco with Bailey, which I still don't understand. You totally screwed him up."

"That's why I'm celibate."

"Celibate, my ass. You fucked that man ten ways from Sunday. You took advantage of a mentally disabled person."

"Hardly. He had high functioning autism. There were things he was very good at, but you also know there were things that he wasn't.

Running a business was never in his future, and Lester knew that. Steven was a reader, an academic, and had Lester left him alone he might have excelled further in academia, but he wanted his son to take over the family business."

"But you saw to it that that would never happen, didn't you?"

"I had everything planned out for him, but Lester wouldn't listen."

"So, you killed him?"

"It was the quickest way to solve the problem. With Lester out of the way, it freed me up to do other things."

"Why did you kill Kristy Yates?"

"You know why. Revenge. Liz got in between me and Steven after Lester's death. She seduced him, and in so doing she took his eyes off of me and what I wanted."

"I don't understand. You waited fifteen years to murder Liz's daughter?"

"No. I waited fifteen years to murder Liz and Steven's daughter. Steven knocked her up, and Liz thought she was going to have this great life, until Steven went off on one of his sexually deviant tangents. He had her locked up for three days, beating and raping her morning, noon, and night. When she got free, she ran as far away from him as possible."

"You triggered that episode with a phone call as I recall."

"Steven liked the lifestyle. He had fun with me at the sex parties and the bondage clubs, so did Liz. That's how they met. It was in one of my orgy parties. I didn't think it would go the way it went. I underestimated her."

"Jesus! They were just kids. You were the mistress. You had control. Why didn't you just end it?"

"I tried."

"I didn't know any of you that well back in those days. I was a nineteen-year-old kid working on my undergrad degree when I met you. I had no idea just how savage you were until years later, and I do know how savage you are, Joann. But to kill Steven and then his child?"

"I will kill Liz, too, but not until she endures the pains of hell while burying her daughter. Steven never knew about Kristy. He was in his own world, and over time, after his father's death, he went deeper and deeper into that world. He was in denial about the things we had done years earlier."

"Why did you kill Steven?"

"He had a flashback."

"A flashback? What the hell do you mean? He didn't do drugs."

"I have worked very hard to keep my back covered when I'm working. I only want those I feel are worthy to see the blood eagle tattoo."

"Steven saw it?"

"Of course, in sex play, but I wear my latex mask when I'm playing mistress or … turning people into angels. Which, by the way, is so much easier with that new robotic machine that your company delivered to me. It does all of the hard work and heavy lifting. I rarely have to use one of my slaves to help me with a kill."

"I had nothing to do with that. Steven got it for you."

Joann smiled an eerie smile as she leaned in over a small candle burning on the table. The flame danced in her eyes, her face in half shadow. "Indeed, he did, and I used it on him and his daughter. The laser on the unit is so precise. I can cut straight through the skin and bone on the back, and the powerful arms pull the rib cage apart from the back, and then I get to look at the beautiful pink flesh of the lungs."

Beverly shook a little in her chair. "I don't want to know anything else."

"You wanted to know why Steven had to die. About a month ago, I wore a blouse with an open back to work as I had a session with one of my subs that night, and I would not have time to change. I always wear a sweater at work, so I thought no big deal. Well, I made a mistake."

"What kind of mistake?"

"I went to the ladies' room, and I didn't know it but Steven was in the men's room. I took off my sweater while I was in there. When I left, I had it in my hand, and Steven came out of the bathroom and saw me from behind."

"How do you know?"

"He cried out, and I put my sweater on and got to him and got him settled down before he threw a full-blown fit."

"And that is why you killed him?"

"He started up again. He started flirting. He started talking to me loudly in the library. He started asking me out and things were getting out of control. You did a great job of getting him to me last night by the way."

"I did what you asked. It's amazing what a good wig and some makeup can do. However, I had no idea you were going to kill him. I would never have done that if I had known what you had planned for him."

"That's why I had you do it the way you did. You did a great job, Beverly. He was well sedated when you brought him to me, and I had a great time with him, and he had a great time with the masked mistress — until he didn't."

"I'm an accessory to murder?"

"No, no. You were doing an ill man a kindness. His life was going nowhere, and if he outed me to anyone it would have destroyed everything I have been working on."

"What do you mean?"

"You know what I mean. The shares in the company that Steven gifted to me. Trevor told me before you arrived that they are worth fifty million dollars. I am coming out, Beverly. I'm going more public in the hopes of getting my true love's attention."

Beverly shook her head. "You don't know what you're doing, Joann."

"I know exactly what I'm doing. With two high-profile murders on the state and federal level, I'm going to attract him. I'm going to get his love and respect."

"You're going to get his attention alright, but I don't see it being what you want."

"We are soulmates, Beverly. Destined to be a couple. Can you imagine it? Me and the Iron Eagle together? He will fall in love with me the minute he lays eyes on me. We can become a power couple."

"A couple of murderers maybe."

"The Eagle extracts justice. I can help him. He can teach me his ways, and I can teach him mine. We are meant for each other. Can't you see that? By getting every law enforcement agency involved, no matter who he is involved with I have covered all the bases."

"I think you're slipping, Joann. You have no idea who the Eagle is. He could be married, single, gay, an introvert. He is a savage and brutal killer. I think that you are inviting the devil to dinner, and he's going to come."

"Perhaps, but he is a good devil. If he is in a relationship, I will get rid of his partner. I doubt he is an introvert. I believe we both operate the same way. He stays low on the radar, so the police and others don't catch him, but I believe he is a loving and caring man who is looking for love and that love is right here."

"Were you wearing your mask when you killed Kristy Yates?"

"Yes, but I always take it off after I have blood eagled my prey, so they can look into my beautiful eyes and see the person who savaged their bodies. A lot of times it's fun because most of my angels know who I am from the library not the dungeon, so when they see my sweet face they're shocked. It can take days, sometimes up to a week to die, and they get to watch me watch them hanging in my cold room, rubbing salt water into their open wounds. Their howls of anguish are music to my ears. I know that the Eagle loves that song, too. Together, we will make beautiful music."

"I think you're losing it. I think you should take your stock and sell it and get the hell out of this city. If you keep this up, you're going to end up dead, along with me and possibly Trevor. Bailey's a wildcard in all of this. She knows your savageness as well, or have you forgotten?"

"Bailey never saw my face, just my tattoo, and she was so traumatized by the whole situation that she isn't going to say a word to anyone. Shit. She's a damn postal worker for Christ's sake, and we see each other almost every day as she delivers mail to the library. It's been over a decade since the dungeon, and I doubt that she will even know about

Steven's death. Even if she does, she's not going to come near any of this. Oh, and on another note, why would Trevor get killed?"

"Oh, I don't know. He hid files on Black's trust from Steven. He manipulated the company for the past several years. He blackmailed Steven over his relationships with Bailey, you, me, Liz. He isn't a great guy, Joann, and he knows you are the one who killed Steven."

"No, he doesn't. He's too self-absorbed with his power grab. All he cares about is money."

"That might be true, but I think Trevor knows a lot more than he is letting on, and he could just as easily be your downfall as well as mine."

"Then I will have to do something about that."

"I'm not getting involved."

"I didn't ask you to."

Beverly stood up and left cash on the table. "Good night, Joann. I sure as hell hope you know what you're doing."

After she left the restaurant, Joann sipped her wine and looked around the empty place. "Perhaps it is you, Beverly, who I need to make into an angel. You know too much."

CHAPTER EIGHT

"She will kill you."

Liz was asleep in an oversized recliner next to Kristy's bed. There had been a few alarms but nothing serious. A nurse was checking Kristy's vitals and charting the information on a computer tablet. Two guards stood outside her room, and a female guard was inside with the two women. She looked at the nurse and asked, "Is that kid going to be okay?"

"Yeah. She's a fighter, and she's strong. I think she'll pull through. It will take some time, but she will get her life and body back." The guard smiled and went back to work on her tablet.

Sara was eating when John arrived at ten thirty. "I see you waited for me," he said.

"Honey, I haven't had anything to eat all day. I'm sorry, but I never know when you're coming home, and I need food."

The chef brought John a plate and poured him a glass of wine and left the room. "So, I take it that Kristy is doing okay?"

"She has a long road to recovery, but she is doing all right. So, you have a female killer who's in love with you, huh?"

"That's what I'm told. This is one messed up case, Sara. This killer wants to flush out the Eagle and thinks he is going to be her lover. I've had some strange cases, but this one makes no sense."

"You've been around for over a decade. You know there are freaks out there who love what you do and are mesmerized by your killings. They don't understand what goes on behind the scenes, but I can see why a woman would be smitten with you."

"You're my wife, Sara. You're smitten with me, and I'm smitten with you. This is a cold-blooded killer, a very, very dangerous killer, and I have a survivor, and I want to be there when you wake her in case she saw her attacker's face or knows her name."

"I will let you know tomorrow if I'm going to bring her out of the coma." They continued eating in silence until Sara asked, "What if this killer learns who you are and that you're married? What do you think will happen?"

"She'll kill you. She'll kill anyone who gets between her and what she wants. Fortunately, only those closest to me know my identity. I don't think this person has anything in her life. Based on what Jim and I learned today, she's a dominatrix who's crossed the line. We have a witness who has seen her nude body and tattoo but not her face."

"Tattoo?"

"Yes. A single large tattoo on her back."

"Of what?"

"A blood eagle."

Jade and Jessica were having a late dinner with Karen and Chris. They were talking about their day and the surgery as Chris stared at his tablet. Karen paused and asked, "Are you okay, Chris?"

"I'm fine. I'm listening. It sounds like you all had quite a day."

Jade laughed. "Well, since we usually open up the dead instead of putting the living back together, it was a hell of a day. It was a rush to be saving a life instead of looking at a corpse and trying to figure out how it died."

Jessica raised her wine glass. "A toast to a day among the living for tomorrow we must go back down among the dead." They toasted, and the women went on conversing as Chris read his tablet.

Bailey Black had been pacing her apartment for several hours. She had a can of Coke in her hand and was mumbling to herself. "Where are you, you bitch? Who are you? You took Steven away. You took my father. Who the fuck are you?" She was still talking when her cellphone rang. "Hello."

"Ms. Bailey Black?"

"Yes."

"Ms. Black, my name is Joann Fontaine. I'm the head librarian for the City of Los Angeles."

Bailey looked at the clock on her dining room wall. It was half past ten. "Do I know you?"

"We have not been formally introduced, but your brother spoke highly of you. He spent his days in my library reading."

"How did you get my phone number?"

"Your brother gave it to me years ago."

"How can I help you?"

"Well, actually, I want to help you. Your brother left quite a collection of books that he owned at the library in our storage for care. He has some real gems and since he has no other family that I'm aware of,

I wanted to call you to see if you would like to see the collection and perhaps pick it up?"

"That's part of my brother's estate, Ms. Fontaine. You would be better off contacting Black Robotics. You can speak to Beverly Hampton. She will know who you need to speak to."

"I see. So, you're not interested in his collection? He has some very, very rare and valuable books."

"No, Ms. Fontaine. I'm not interested in the books. Why are you calling me so late?"

"I was close to your brother."

"I know he had a huge crush on you, but that you shot him down multiple times."

"Indeed, I did, and I feel bad about that. He was a kind, sweet man, and I should have treated him better." Bailey burst out in laughter. "What's so funny, Ms. Black?"

"You really didn't know my brother at all, Ms. Fontaine."

"I don't understand."

"That's good," Bailey said, "because if you did, I would want to know more about you."

Bailey hung up the phone. Joann was sitting in a club chair, nude, holding the phone in her hands. "Well, Bailey doesn't know who I am by voice, so that's good, but I think that Beverly is right. She needs to be taken out before she remembers something and talks."

Jim and Cindy were in bed. She was resting her head on his chest and both were out of breath. "Wow! What inspired that?"

"It was a long, violent day. I needed a release."

"Well, Jimmy, you released twice by my count. That was great."

Jim laughed and asked, "And how was your day?"

"Up until about an hour ago pretty much same old same old. Karen was out a large part of the day, so I picked up some of her patient load and dealt with my own. That poor little girl who had been so brutalized. I don't know how the teams got her put back together."

"Modern medicine. They can do just about anything."

"Any leads on who this killer is?"

"It's been less than twenty-four hours, Cindy. We rarely get leads in cases like this that fast. I got one hell of an education on some twisted family matters, though. Every time I think I have seen or heard it all, someone pops out of the woodwork with something so nuts it just puts me on tilt."

He got up, grabbed a cigarette, and walked to the deck. Cindy got up as well and asked while pulling on a robe, "Would you like a drink, Jim?"

"That would be great, honey."

Cindy poured two glasses of scotch and brought one to Jim then sat down on a lounge chair. "So, do you want to talk about what you heard today?"

"No."

"I learn a lot of sick stuff in my job, too, Jimmy. Incest, pedophiles, rapists, twisted sexual desires, and fantasies."

"If these people are engaging in that type of conduct, you're supposed to report them."

"They fantasize about it and then tell me sometimes to see my reaction. Others feel guilty that they could think that way and think there is something wrong with them."

"If someone is having fantasies about having sex with kids or raping people, that, to me, is a problem. Fantasy lines get crossed all the time, and the next thing you know someone has gone and done it."

"I won't say it doesn't happen but not as much as you might think, Jim."

"Well, I see the real thing every day, and I can tell you if these people haven't been fantasizing before they did these things then they were just born sick."

"You have a good point. There are people who are just born sick. If I had a person in my office I felt was reliving real events, I would call the authorities right away. The people who are born sick don't know they are sick. They don't seek treatment, and for those who get caught in the case of pedophilia and rape, those people can't be cured."

"Have you ever had a patient cross the line?"

"Yes."

"Want to talk about that?"

"His name was Thomas Marker."

Jim dropped the cigarette out of his mouth onto his bare legs. "Ouch, ouch. Son of a bitch! Thomas Marker the serial killer mortician who was in bed with Simon Barstow?"

"Yes."

"He was your patient?"

"He was, and I listened to him fantasize on my couch for two years before the discovery of his crimes."

"Discovery of his crimes? That son of a bitch raped, tortured, and emasculated teenage boys for years. He had his own genital collection in an attic storage space. I know. I was there. I saw it. I had my investigators tagging the specimens after Marker was killed."

"I missed all the signs, Jim. I took the discovery of his killings very hard and very personally. I almost left the field after that."

Jim had moved near Cindy, who was crying. "You could never have known, Cindy. Marker was a pure sociopath. He was a smooth talker who had a way of getting what he wanted and disarming people."

"He didn't disarm you, did he?"

"I'm not the one who got to him. The Eagle found out about his sins, and he died badly as a result."

"But not before hundreds of young men and boys had been murdered?"

"No. Marker had been killing for decades. He had access to a crematorium. There was no evidence outside of the jars in his attic. If it hadn't been for the Eagle recognizing Marker's car one night on a crime scene, and the only reason there was a crime scene was due to Marker losing the access he had to the crematoriums, there is a good chance the Eagle would never have caught him, and he would still be killing today."

"That's cold comfort, Jim. When I read the list of missing children that were attributed to Marker, I got physically ill. I deal with sick people every day. The Marker case taught me a lot, and I am very, very careful when I take on a new patient and do an intake. I'm a psychologist. I have a Ph.D. in philosophy and then spent four years training under a psychiatrist, who as you know, is an M.D."

"Why didn't you go to medical school like Karen and become a psychiatrist?"

"I didn't have the money for that. Kevin was little, and I needed to finish my education, so I could support him and myself. It takes years of schooling to become an M.D. and even more schooling to specialize in matters of the mind. In the Marker case, even a trained psychiatrist would have missed the mark or at least that's what I was told. Anyway, it is water under the bridge, and I have come to grips with it."

"Well, the case still gives me nightmares, but then so do so many other cases."

"You've seen a lot in your years in law enforcement. How do you cope with it? Do you see a therapist?"

Jim raised his scotch glass. "I get through it with the help of this golden elixir and a good cigarette."

"Both of which can kill you."

"We are all going to die from something. When I was shot as a U.S. Marshal, I saw my life pass before my eyes. It was a short life then, but it was still like watching every scene and emotion in my life passing by in slow motion. I have only had that experience once even with my close calls with the Eagle and doing my job. It changed me. It made me unafraid of death."

"Fearing death is a waste of time. We're all heading there."

"Most people are afraid of it. I'm not, and I agree that it is a waste of time to fear the inevitable. It did awaken me to loving life and enjoying all the good things in it. I know I bitch a lot, and I'm cynical. Police work has made me that way. However, I do live my life by my terms, and the reason I do was because some asshole bail jumper shot me, and the Eagle saved me." Jim finished off his drink. "Let's catch some shut eye. In a few hours we have to go back to the real world, and it is one fucked up place."

Trevor was working in his office. It was three thirty a.m., and he was reading over the Black trust documents as well as all of the other paperwork related to the family history. He had nodded off a few times and was about to go home when his cellphone rang.

"Trevor, it's Joann."

"Joann. What are you doing up at this hour?"

"I couldn't sleep. I just keep seeing Steven's body in the bushes when I close my eyes."

"Have you tried taking a sleeping pill?"

"I don't believe in pills. I was wondering if you wouldn't mind stopping by my condo."

"Do you think that's a good idea, Joann? We have no history, and I know you're celibate, but it is things like this that can turn into things you regret later."

"I'm not worried about that, Trevor. I thought you might like to see my angel collection and just talk."

"You have an angel collection?"

"Oh, yes. A very beautiful one. They keep me uplifted when things are tough."

"I really need to get some sleep, Joann. Can you make it on your own tonight?"

"I really wish you would come over. I have a guest room, and you can sleep in there if you wish after we talk."

"Okay. I will be there in a half hour."

"Thank you, Trevor. I really appreciate this. I have no one else."

Trevor hung up the phone and turned off his computer. He smiled and said, "Well, well, well. It looks like I'm going to get laid."

CHAPTER NINE

"You are now one with the angels."

Trevor arrived at Joann's condo at four and was greeted by a friendly doorman who let him in and then pressed an express elevator button. "Ms. Fontaine is in the penthouse. This elevator will open right into her foyer. There will be a call button next to the elevator doors. Please press it. Good night, sir."

The elevator doors opened into a grand foyer with marble floors and statuary all around it. There was a button next to the elevator that read 'Call.' He pressed it and in a matter of seconds Joann appeared in the foyer.

"When you say you're going to be somewhere at a certain time, you aren't kidding." Trevor had a shocked smile on his face as Joann stood in the entry nude. She walked up to him and kissed his lips then proceeded to take him by the hand and walk him into a dark corridor.

The condo was wall to wall windows with views that spanned three-hundred-sixty degrees of downtown LA. She pulled him into a bedroom then proceeded to undo his pants. Trevor didn't say a word as Joann seduced him, and in a matter of minutes, she had his manhood in her mouth, and he was groaning. He could see her head moving up and down on him, and he just threw his head back and went with it. He orgasmed hard and could hear Joann swallowing his semen as it flowed out of him, then she rose, pushed him down on the bed, and spread her thighs over his face. "Eat me."

Joann writhed and moved her pelvis across Trevor's lips and face, and the two went back and forth for about an hour until they collapsed.

"I thought you were celibate."

"I lied. I tell that lie to keep men I don't like away. I get hit on all the time, and it gets old."

The room was dark except for a light glowing from the bathroom.

"Is it okay if I use the bathroom?"

"Of course. You must also be thirsty. I have just about every type of beverage. Would you like something?"

Trevor called out from the bathroom, "I could go for a sparkling water."

"No problem. Do you like lemon?"

"Sure. That would be great." He finished up in the bathroom and walked back into the bedroom where Joann was seated at a small table with a bottle of water on it and two glasses.

"Please sit and enjoy a beverage with me."

"I have to tell you, Joann. I have fantasized about you several times, even while coming over here tonight, but you are way more in reality."

"Well, thank you. I know how to let my hair down. All librarians aren't old maids."

"I'm well aware of that. I have slept with a few and most tend to be quite kinky."

"So, you like it kinky, huh?"

Trevor took a drink of his water and smiled. "Indeed, I do. This is really good water."

"I'm glad you like it, so what kind of kinky do you like?"

"Everything. Work keeps me so busy that I rarely get a chance to do the things I did when I was in college. I used to hit the sex club scene, BDSM, group sex, pretty much anything you can imagine."

"I see, so are you a top or a bottom?"

"I cross play, so I can be both. What about you?"

"Oh, I'm a top, baby. A mistress of the dungeon. I work hard, and I play hard."

Joann stood up and removed her robe then turned her back to Trevor and raised her arms in the air. "Good God. What is that?"

"My tattoo. It's still a work in progress. What do you think?"

"It's horrific. What is it?"

"A blood eagle. You haven't seen one, have you?"

"No, and it is quite disturbing. This is a side of you I would never have expected."

"Oh, I'm full of surprises, Trevor, just full of them. As I stated, I work hard and play hard."

"The play hard I can vouch for, so where is this angel collection you wanted to show me?"

"In a minute, dear. Drink your water. You are really sweating."

Trevor continued to sip his water, and the two made small talk for about ten minutes, then Trevor suddenly said, "What is in this water?"

"Feeling a little sleepy, are you?" Trevor never responded as his head hit the table.

Jade and Jessica were in the morgue early as they had missed the day before. The night crew was putting bodies in coolers, and Jessica was looking over the night's intake forms. "I swear, Jade, this city is getting more violent by the day. I know that the cops, politicians, and media want to spread the news that LA is a safe city. I know they screw with the real numbers that they then feed to the media, and they feed to the public, but we know the truth."

"How many last night?"

"Twenty-five."

"We are understaffed and overworked, Jess. The city isn't giving us the resources we need to do the job, and with twenty to fifty bodies a day coming in and the wide range of deaths, what used to take days is taking months."

Jessica nodded as one of the doctors walked into the office. "Jade, I know you give priority to the Sheriff's Department and the feds, but the local PD and families of victims are revolting against us. I have a backlog of cases that can choke a horse. Something has to give, or I'm going to have to tender my resignation."

Jade sat down. "Dr. Chu, I understand your frustration, and we are working as fast as we can to get more people and more funding. The board of supervisors doesn't take our work seriously. They don't understand what it takes to solve cases, especially given the multiple manners of death people suffer where there is no outward trauma. Drug overdoses are one of the biggest ones. They don't understand that the only way we can give a proper cause of death requires not only an autopsy but toxicology reports and what used to take weeks can take six months. Please be patient with us. We will get you more resources."

The doctor left the office, and Jessica looked at Jade. "We are going to lose him and more staff. We are really screwed."

"The city is playing with fire. We take all precautions and follow the letter of the law. If they keep ignoring our needs, something is going to slip through, a virus, bacteria, hell, a man-made substance that could kill millions, and it will be the direct fault of the city board of supervisors, and when it happens, they will scatter like roaches."

Trevor was moaning as his nude body was raised over the blades of the robot. His arms and legs were speared by the unit. Joann was standing off to his right, and he raised his head to see her looking at him and asked, "Why are you doing this?"

"Well, you know about the stock that Steven gifted me, and I just can't have you taking me down."

"Why would Steven give you stock?"

"I'm not going to get into that." The machine came to life, and two laser sights beamed down on Trevor's spine. He screamed, and she laughed. "That laser is cutting through your skin and ribcage to open you up. I'm going to make you one of my angels, Trevor."

Trevor was screaming as the lasers sliced through his back. As each cut was made, the ribs would pop up in his back, and he would scream louder. When the final cuts were done, the robotic arms grabbed both sides of his back and pulled the ribs open, exposing his lungs. His body slid back along the table, and Joann stood next to him. "Beautiful lungs. I see you're not a smoker." She took several tools and then pressed them around his lungs. "You're going to feel a hell of a lot of pressure."

She pulled the steel instruments until Trevor's lungs were out of his body and on his back. He lost his breath and ability to scream. Joann took some salt water and rubbed it into the wounds as the machine cut a slit at the base of Trevor's back and implanted a steel brace. "That's specially designed to give you flight."

Trevor was losing consciousness, but Joann injected him with a large syringe, and he jerked back to alertness. He was working to breathe and speak. "You're out of your mind."

"Hardly. This will keep you quiet and buy me time to find out what the feds want with the trust documents. It will also allow me to sell my shares through a shell company. I have big plans, Trevor, huge plans."

The machine gripped Trevor's body as he fought for air and a voice. The robotics turned him right side up and then lifted him to a waiting rack just outside the cold room. Joann had a remote control in her hands and was using a joystick to move his body to the hooks on the steel rack and then lowered him onto them. Once he was secured, she released his arms and legs, and his body weight pulled down on the bracket, and he let out a high-pitched scream. "Sorry about that. The shock of the pressure can be a bit—stunning." She wheeled the rack into the room with the others and when Trevor saw four other people torn to pieces, their lungs slowly expanding and contracting in a bloody dance, he fought to scream. "You'll want to conserve your energy, Trevor. I want you with me as long as possible. Welcome to my angel collection. You are now one with the angels."

John and Chris got into their office just before seven. "Did you read over the trust documents?" asked Chris.

"I did, and I don't really see anything out of the ordinary. Have you read them?"

"I read them last night while Jade and Jessica were over for dinner."

"Did you see anything?"

"I saw a ten percent transfer of stock gifted to Steven Black right after his father died and then another transfer from Black to an unknown person."

"I saw that, too. It's not uncommon in businesses like these to see this type of behavior. He could have made the transfer for himself. His father could have set it up before he died. I don't see the stock ever having been sold, so who knows."

"You always tell me to follow the money, John. Ten percent of a company the size of Black Robotics is significant. It's publicly traded on the exchanges, and at its last close yesterday that ten percent was worth about fifty million dollars. That's a lot of money. It begs the question—who has the stock, and what are they going to do with it?"

"You have a point. Let's pay Trevor a visit. He's pissed, but he has no reason not to talk to us. Perhaps he can shed some light on this."

Beverly got to her office just before eight. Her assistant entered and asked how she was doing. "I'm tired, Tracy, really, really tired."

"Didn't get a good night's sleep, huh?" Beverly shook her head. "How about a strong cup of coffee, boss?"

"That would be great. Thank you."

Beverly unpacked her laptop and tablet and started to set up for the day when Tracy buzzed her. "Beverly, Ms. Bailey Black is here to see you."

"Really? I will be right out." Bailey was dressed in her postal service uniform when Beverly came to the front office. She reached out her hand, and Bailey shook it. "It's been a long time, Bailey."

"Indeed. Is there somewhere we can talk?"

Beverly led Bailey to her office, and the two sat down. "What brings you to see me?"

"Steven's murder."

"What about it?"

"When Steven and I fooled around before our father died, he took me to several party clubs, one of which was run by a dominatrix who only went by Mistress."

"I remember that person."

"You do?"

"Yes."

"Where does she live?"

"I don't know. She ran a club in Hollywood where Steven would go, and I recall you being taken there a few times. Why are you interested in her?"

"She had a full back tattoo that she called a blood eagle. I was looking up the term and discovered some terrifying facts about it."

"Oh? Like what?"

"The blood eagle was a Viking way of killing their most hated enemies after battle. It was a barbaric way to kill and a horrific way to die."

"From what I know about the act, it was a myth."

"Well, it might have been myth, but it is now reality. Steven was murdered using the blood eagle technique, and I think that Mistress is involved."

"That's a pretty bold statement and a serious accusation."

"Do you know of anyone else that has that type of tattoo or passion about such a means of killing? She talked about it in sessions with me and Steven. She was obsessed with blood and often licked it off my back after a whipping while whispering to me that I tasted good."

"I don't recall any of that."

"Were you in her dungeon as a guest or victim?"

"Yes."

"Do you know who she is? What her name is?"

"No."

"No? How could you not know who this person is? You were there. You knew Steven. You knew who we were to each other and how twisted that was."

"Bailey, I was nineteen or twenty. I was a kid in college who was introduced to that underground world. It opened my eyes to alternate sex acts and ways of getting pleasure through pain, but I didn't like it. I didn't know Mistress. I never saw her face as she always wore a latex mask. Steven was involved with her, and as far as I know you never saw her face."

"That's why I'm here. There is a lot of bad blood between us, but I think that if we work together, we can find this chick. I believe she is the one who killed Steven, and I think she has or will kill others."

"I wish I could help you, Bailey, but I have no idea who she was. It was a long time ago, and my life has changed incredibly since those days."

"Indeed. You now run my family's multibillion dollar business. With Steven dead and no heir, the trust will be kicking in, and I can't imagine how that is going to work."

"I know nothing about the trust, Bailey. Trevor Craig is handling all of that. He will give direction over the next few weeks. So much has happened so quickly. I am lost in all of this as well."

"I don't see how. My brother and I have been out of the company from day one. You and my brother had your fling, which didn't go well. Perhaps I should talk to the police. Perhaps they might know more."

"I wouldn't rule it out. If I were you, that's where I would go."

Bailey stood up to leave but paused and looked Beverly up and down. "I think you know who Mistress is, Beverly."

She didn't respond as Bailey walked out of the office, but she picked up the phone and said, "Joann, it's Beverly. I just had a visit from Bailey Black."

"Interesting that she would call on you. What did she want?"

"Information on you. She wanted to know if I knew your name or had any information about you."

"What did you tell her?"

"No, of course. I told her I only met you a few times and that I never saw your face or knew your name."

"It would seem that Bailey is trying to do her own investigation into Steven's death."

"She's going to the cops."

"How do you know that?"

"She told me."

"I see, well, let her knock herself out."

"Aren't you worried?"

"No. She doesn't know who I am. You have said you know nothing about me, so what's to worry about?"

"She thinks you're Steven's killer. She also remembers your tattoo as well as things you did to her years ago. If she tells the cops that I was in that dungeon a few times, that's going to get me a visit."

"I really don't feel that's an issue right now. I have slowed the trust investigation, so that won't be a concern. I think it's time to sell my shares before this all gets public and the value drops."

"And just how did you slow the trust investigation?"

"I have my ways, now find a broker who can move the shares under the radar. You have my account in the Caymans, right?"

"Yes. It was part of the information that Steven gave me a few years ago."

"Sell my shares as soon as possible and then have the funds transferred off shore to my account."

"Have you heard anything on Kristy Yates' murder?"

"No."

"It's been two days. Doesn't it bother you that there is nothing in the news about it?"

"No. It's a federal investigation now. The Secret Service and FBI will be handling her death. The feds aren't going to advertise that the daughter of one of their own was murdered so heinously. They are going to try and profile and find the killer before going public."

"I don't know, Joann. Something feels wrong about the Yates kid."

"Well, I can talk to her mother."

"Are you out of your mind? You think that won't send up red flags?"

"Not at all. Liz doesn't know I am the mistress. She comes into the library all the time, and I speak to her often. I'll give it a day or two and then give her a call. She has a book that is overdue and when I speak to her, I will see if she tells me anything about Kristy. The kid was in a lot of programs here in my branch and at her mother's local branch in Beverly Hills."

"I don't know how you have been able to stay in plain sight all of these years with no one questioning you."

"It's easy. I don't put my victims on parade. I'm not your typical serial killer. I kill under the radar and then get rid of my angels privately, so no one knows what I am doing. Steven and Kristy were the exceptions to my rule."

"And why is that?"

"I wanted to send a message first to you with Steven's transformation that no one is out of my reach and, second, to hurt Liz for the pain she caused me by having Steven's kid. Those are the only two public killings outside of Lester Black in over a decade. Now that they are finished, I will get my money and move on with my life."

"And the killings?"

"Oh, Beverly, I will always have my angel collection. That won't change. I have my two slaves who help me with the bodies, and I have no worry about them as I keep them locked up and beat them regularly. They are loyal to me to the death. Once the cash is in my hands, I will drop off the radar again never to be seen or heard from."

"What about the Iron Eagle?"

"Oh, he will find me. I have no worries about that. And when he does, my life will be complete. I have given him two high profile deaths to investigate. I know he is out there hunting, and I can't wait to meet him."

"I have a feeling you are going to meet the Eagle; however, I don't think it is going to work out the way you are hoping."

"I could not bear being rejected by the Eagle. To reject me is to die. He will become my lover, my partner, my soulmate. You will see; he has no other choice."

CHAPTER TEN

*"I understand that you found
Steven Black's body yesterday?"*

ara was looking over Kristy's chart and smiling. Liz was seated in
her chair and asked, "Is that a smile of satisfaction?"

"Yeah. Kristy is looking very, very strong. The surgery has gone
well, and I think we can start to bring her out of the coma this afternoon."

"Why not right now?"

"The FBI wants to be here when she wakes up. They're hoping she
will be able to ID her attempted killer."

"After all of this trauma, do you really think that Kristy is going to
remember anything?"

"I have no idea, Liz, but it is important to get as much information
from her as we can right away. The longer she is in a coma and the more
she heals, the more likely it is that she will lose memory and that could
be costly and dangerous for her."

"Dangerous?"

"There have been no media leaks on your daughter's condition. The killer only knows what he saw the last time he dealt with her body. If the killer learns she is still alive and that she can speak, he will most likely do anything in order to get to her and kill her."

"But that's what the FBI is here to prevent."

"People die while under protection all the time, Liz. If people have the right contacts, the right clearance, they can get to anyone, and if they do, they could kill your daughter right under our noses, and we might never be the wiser. It is dreadfully important that you not speak about her being alive if you're asked about her. Don't comment, but if someone close to you asks, just tell them she's dead."

"This is turning into an even bigger nightmare. My baby is alive, but I must tell people she's dead? There is a killer out there who thinks she's dead, and I don't know if any person that I speak to is the enemy."

"That's about the size of it. I deal with this all the time. John is now the Deputy Director of the Los Angeles field office of the FBI, but he was a special agent for years. I have seen the good and bad in these cases. You have to treat Kristy as dead to anyone you speak to until John and his people can talk to her. You also have to worry about your safety."

"My safety? What about it?"

"This might not be some random act, Liz. This might be targeted at you and Kristy for a reason. There is no way to know for sure, but I have a feeling that this killer has you in his sights, and Kristy might just be the beginning of your suffering."

"I don't like this shit, Sara. I don't like it at all."

"Neither do I. There was another killing yesterday morning that fits the M.O. of what Kristy went through."

"There was?"

Sara nodded and said, "The body was found outside the main branch of the Los Angeles Public Library downtown."

"Do you know who the victim was?"

"I'm not at liberty to say at this moment, but it was a middle-aged man, and he was torn apart just like Kristy."

"I need to know who was killed, Sara."

"Why?"

"Because I need to know, and I need to know now!"

Jim and Sam were sitting in their car in front of Trevor Craig's offices. "What time did John say he would be here?" Sam asked.

"Nine. We're a few minutes early."

"Did you get a chance to read over the trust documents?"

"No. He hasn't released them yet."

"Then why the hell are we here?"

"I don't fuckin' know, Sam, but if John wants us here there's a reason."

"He has his case, Jim, and we have ours. At least his case is still alive."

Jim saw John's truck pull up behind him, and he and Sam stepped out. John and Chris got out of the truck, and Jim asked, "What the fuck are we doing here, John?"

"I read over the trust documents last night."

"Okay, that's swell, but what does that have to do with us?"

"Mr. Black had a substantial interest in his father's company. He held a twenty-five percent stake as well as a ten percent stake that he gifted to another party."

"Okay. Who got the stock?"

"That's literally the million-dollar question, and Trevor Craig has the answer."

He pointed to the building entrance, and the four walked in, showed their IDs, and went up to Trevor's offices.

"Help me. Somebody please help me." Trevor's voice was soft as he looked around the cooler where several other bodies hung around him. He could see the steam coming off of the bodies and the lungs on the ones in front of him rising and lowering slowly. He hung in the air. "Oh, God, please help me."

A weak female voice out of view answered Trevor. "God can't help you. No one can help you. You're dead."

"I'm sorry, Director Swenson, but Mr. Craig is not in the office this morning."

"When do you expect him?"

Trevor's assistant was looking over her calendar then looked at the four people standing in front of her desk. "To be honest, he should be here. He is always in the office between six thirty and seven a.m., but he has not come in yet."

"Does Mr. Craig live in Howard Cohen's condo on the top of this building?"

"No. No one lives up there. It's been vacant since Mr. Cohen took his life. Mr. Craig lives in a condo complex at nine hundred West Olympic Boulevard in the Ritz Carlton Building. It's a very nice place and allows him to have all the amenities of a hotel while living in his own condo."

"Have you called his home or cellphone."

"No but let me try him." The young woman dialed several numbers and hung up. "Just voicemail. Let me call the Ritz." She dialed yet another number and said, "Jenny Graph, please. This is Ester from Trevor Craig's office." There were a few moments of silence. "Good morning, Jenny. This is Ester. How are you this morning?"

"Good, Ester. I'm just coming off the night shift. How can I help you?"

"I'm trying to locate Mr. Craig. Have you spoken to him since last night?"

"I'm afraid not. He never called down for his usual late dinner. Have you tried all of his numbers?"

"I have and no answer. It's so unusual for him not to be in the office by this hour. He has no court dates today or depositions. His calendar is wide open."

"I don't know what to tell you, Ester. I will leave word with the front desk to have a message left from you and ask the staff to call your office if they see him."

"Thank you, Jenny. Have a nice day."

"Well, Director, I have no idea where Mr. Craig is. I can call you or have him call you when he comes in."

John handed her a card as did Sam. John looked around the office then at Ester and said, "Please have Mr. Craig call me or Sheriff Pritchard when he arrives." He paused for a moment. "If we hadn't shown up this morning, what time would you have become concerned?"

"Oh, that's a hard question to answer. While this is unusual, it's not unheard of, Director. Mr. Craig is a single man, so he could be out. If I hadn't heard from him by the end of the day, then I would be concerned. He always checks in multiple times in a day if he is out."

"Concerned enough to file a missing persons report?"

"No. I would report it to the partners, and they would handle it from there."

The four thanked her and left the building. Jim took a cigarette from his top left pocket, lit it outside the building, and took a deep drag off of it. John and Chris were at their truck, and Jim was standing near the trunk of his cruiser looking around.

"What are thinking, Jim?" John asked.

"Thinking? I think that Mr. Craig is gone. He has been disappeared."

"Disappeared?"

"Yeah. He's dead, and I don't think you're going to find his body."

Bailey arrived for her route and was sorting mail and putting it in her truck when her supervisor stopped by. Bailey was moving quickly as she was ten minutes behind schedule. "Good morning, Bailey. You're a little late."

"I'm sorry about that. I had family business to deal with."

"Not a problem. I'm sure you will get the mail delivered on time."

Bailey threw the last box of mail into her truck and headed out of the station. She started her deliveries downtown and worked her way through the city until she arrived at the public library. The mail boxes for the library were outside, but there were always boxes of materials that had to be delivered to the library's shipping area. She pulled her truck around the back and up to a small loading dock then opened the back of her truck and began moving boxes onto the platform. Two male workers greeted her and began helping her get the boxes out of the truck. By the time she was finished, she was dripping with sweat and had a handful of letters that needed to be signed for; two of them were addressed to Joann Fontaine. One of the men stated he would sign, but she told him that Fontaine must sign for them in her presence.

Joann was sitting in the lunch room eating a snack and reading a journal when Bailey walked in. Joann smiled and said, "It's so nice to see you, Bailey. We probably had a lot of material today, huh?"

"Yeah, Joann. I have two registered letters that you must sign for." Joann pulled a pen out of her hair and signed the documents. Bailey ripped off the portion for the sender and handed the letters back to her. "That was a strange call from you last night about Steven's books."

"I'm sorry. It was a courtesy. You're here, though, so would you like to see his collection?"

"I wasn't interested last night, and I'm not interested today. I understand that you found Steven's body yesterday."

Joann got teary-eyed. "I did. I didn't know it was him until later in the day. I am beyond devastated."

"I bet. When was the last time you spoke to Steven?"

"Yesterday evening. He was reading a Joyce work, and we were talking about the novel."

"Did he seem upset or have any behavior issues?"

"Not at all. He was in good spirits. He asked me out again, and I refused him."

"I know the game, Joann. You don't need to go into it with me. You have talked to law enforcement?"

"Yes. I know little but answered all of their questions. When was the last time you spoke to your brother?"

"It's not important. What matters is that he was brutally murdered. I know my brother had a sick side but nothing that would have deserved that type of torture and agony."

"I didn't really know your brother outside of the library, so I wouldn't know about that. I don't think anyone deserves to die like that, and I am devastated at the savagery of the torture your brother endured."

Bailey pulled her mail bag up on her shoulder and stood up straight. "I know you're no saint, Joann. You want people to think you are, but you're not. If I find out you had anything to do with Steven's death, the law will be the least of your worries."

"Are you threatening me?"

"No, I'm promising you. You will suffer as my brother suffered only a thousand times worse."

Bailey left, and Joann sat back in her chair. Once she knew Bailey was gone and she was alone, she muttered to herself quietly, "So, Bailey likes to make threats. Perhaps she will be my next angel. She's one person that won't be missed." She paused then looked at the clock on the wall. It was ten after twelve. She shook her head lightly and said, "Could it be? Could it be that I have been wrong about the Eagle's sex? Could it be that the Eagle is actually a woman? That the Eagle is Bailey Black? Dear God, no!"

CHAPTER ELEVEN

"No, lie to me. I love it."

"I'm going to start bringing Kristy Yates out of her coma at three, John."

Sara was on one of the hospital phones speaking to him outside of Kristy's room.

"Okay, it's one thirty. We'll grab some lunch and then come over. Please don't wake her until we are there. Has there been a changing of the guard on her security?"

"Yes. Three fresh agents are here." Sara paused, "John, Liz Yates wants to know the name of the other victim."

"Did you tell her?"

"No, but she is very animated and has been calling several phone numbers trying to reach someone."

"Keep it to yourself. We'll tell her when we get there." John hung up the line and looked at Chris. "Interesting possible development. Liz Yates is very distraught over the body found yesterday at the library and wants to know who it is."

"Why is that interesting?"

"I don't know. It was in Sara's voice. Liz was very, very upset and was trying to call someone whom she couldn't reach."

"Do you think there is a connection to Black?"

"I don't know, but we are going to find out. Call the office and get our best sketch artist over to the hospital. Sara is going to bring the girl out of her coma at three. I will call Jim and Sam. I have a feeling things are about to get interesting."

Chris started laughing. "Like things aren't already? Jesus, John! We have one dead, another saved, and a psycho out there doing God only knows what. Trevor Craig has disappeared; Jim thinks he's dead. You have an admirer who is also a brutal killer. How the fuck much more interesting could this case get?"

Jim and Sam were sitting in their spot at Santiago's having lunch when John called. Jim spoke quickly and hung up.

"What was that all about?"

"Sara is going to wake the Yates girl at three, so John wants us there."

"It's only one thirty, so we have time to finish our lunch."

Jim nodded, cracking open a bottle of beer and then taking a bite of his sandwich. "So, what's going on with you and Sandy?"

"We're taking it slow."

"Your house will be finished this weekend. When are you planning to move in?"

"I haven't been able to think that far ahead, Jim."

"You better start thinking about it. What about Sandy? Will she be moving in with you?"

"No."

"Why the fuck not?"

"Because I'm not ready. I am in love with her and she with me, but I'm just not ready to start down that road."

"Getting cold feet after professing your love for her?"

"No. There's just so much going on between my term ending next year and you preparing to run for office again. I need my space while I think things through."

"I heard Sandy asked you about applying to work at the Bureau."

"Yeah." Sam cracked a beer open and took a few swigs. "I think that if I joined the Bureau I would be jumping from the pan into the fire."

"How so?"

"John is going to end up in Washington if President Hernandez gets a second term, which looks like a no brainer. If John takes the job as the FBI Director and is confirmed, I'm sure he will take a small team of agents from LA with him. You're running for Sheriff again, and your poll numbers look great. I just don't know that making the jump from local law enforcement to federal is a good move."

"I did it. I went from the U.S. Marshals Service to the LA County Sheriff's Department. John made the leap from LAPD to the Bureau. What are you afraid of?"

"Honestly?"

"No. Lie to me. I love it."

"I'm afraid of what this city is going to be like without the Eagle. I'm worried about cases coming into our offices that we can't solve and crime rates that are relatively low increasing due to the Eagle's absence."

Jim finished off his beer and then lit a cigarette. "Sam, I have been a cop a long time, even back before there was an Eagle. There will always be someone to step into those shoes. You don't really think that John is going to remain the Eagle forever, do you?"

"I never thought about it. I suppose that sooner or later John is going to get caught, killed, or move on."

"He's grooming several successors."

"Several?"

"Yes. They don't know they are being groomed, but he knows what he's doing and when the time comes, assuming he is alive, he will pass the torch to another vigilante inside law enforcement and move on."

"And if he is killed before he can do that?"

Jim shrugged, blowing smoke from his lungs. "Then he dies. He knows the risks, but if he dies before dealing with the person to take over for him that person will rise to the occasion, and there will be a new killer keeping the worst of the worst off the streets. You can't worry about it. You just need to keep learning and keep moving."

"And if I decide to leave law enforcement altogether?"

"You might, but you would be so goddamned miserable. You're not one for sitting on the sidelines watching the news every night and seeing the shit that's happening in this city and doing nothing about it."

"I might leave the state."

"That's your call not mine. For now, we have our jobs to do, so let's get over to the hospital and see what new information we can glean from this kid and her mother."

Sara was working with two other doctors on Kristy when John and Chris arrived. John ordered his men out of the room and had the sketch artist sitting ready as Sara began to inject medications. Before she could get the first one in, Liz stopped her. "Sara told me that another body had been discovered yesterday with the same torture that my daughter had."

"That's correct, Ms. Yates," John said. "The body of a middle-aged man was discovered by the head librarian at the downtown branch of the Los Angeles Public Library."

"Do you know the identity of the man?"

"Yes"

"Tell me."

"Why?"

Liz started to tear up and screamed, "JUST TELL ME!"

Everyone in the room jumped except John, who was about to speak when Jim and Sam arrived.

"Well, someone is pissed off in here," said Jim.

"Ms. Yates wants to know the identity of the man found dead yesterday by the same means as her daughter."

"So tell her."

"The victim's name was Steven Black."

Liz began to shutter and shake as she lost all control of her body and fell out of the chair to the floor. "Jesus Christ! She's having a seizure. Give me ten milligrams of diazepam, stat." Sara barked out the orders. Once the injection was administered, Liz began to calm down. John had taken a seat near her as the others stood near the entrance. Liz was a bit loopy as the medication took effect, but she was able to get back into her chair as tears were streaming down her face.

John waited for her to regain her composure and once she had he asked, "I take it you knew Mr. Black?"

"Yes, I did. Very, very well."

"Can you tell me how you knew him?"

"He is Kristy's father."

Every jaw dropped in the room. Even Jim stood in stunned silence. Liz propped herself up in her chair, and Sara was standing next to her and asked, "Does Kristy know who her father is?"

"No."

"Is there a reason for that?"

"Yes."

John eased in and put his hand on Liz's. "And why is it that your daughter doesn't know who her father is?"

"He was insane. He got me pregnant at a time in my life when I was a freewheeling swinger. I was exploring my sexuality, and we met at a swinger's bar and started up a relationship. When I learned that I was pregnant, I went to him and told him. He became irate and accused me of trying to trap him to get to his money. He argued that I told him I was on birth control, which I was, but I told him that it wasn't foolproof. He beat me and raped me over a three-day period, and when I was able to get free, I ran for my life. I had never planned to see him again."

"Did you get a paternity test?"

"Yes, and it came back positive that he was the father."

"Was Mr. Black's father still alive when you learned you were pregnant?"

"Yes. He was killed about six months later."

"Did Mr. Black or his father make any provisions for Kristy?"

"No. After that brutal weekend, I feared for my life and the life of my child. Lester Black was happy and sad about the child. He was concerned it would have autism like Stephen. He did learn before his death that I had all of the genetic testing done before birth and that the child was a girl and appeared to be perfectly normal. After his death, Steven went off the deep end and threw himself into books, detaching from reality. He would spend his days at the library reading and isolating himself. He was fascinated with the librarian, Joann Fontaine. He was head over heels for her, but I don't really know what came out of it."

John was still sitting next to her and said, "Liz, I have a very important question to ask you."

"Go ahead."

"When you were in this lifestyle, were there others who you met and who went through it with you?"

Liz cleared her throat and opened her eyes wide. "There was a small group of us that hung out. I got involved with Steven through Bailey Black and Beverly Hampton. There was a third woman, but I don't know her name. She was a mistress at a private dungeon club in Hollywood. She always wore different types of latex masks, but she worked nude other than a pair of thigh high black leather boots. She was a mean bitch. Really, really mean, and Steven had fallen under her spell after our tryst. I only went to the club a few times, but she was always beating men and women, and they were paying her to do it to them."

"Do you recall any markings on her? Tattoos, piercings, brands?"

"Oh, yes! She had the most hideous tattoo that covered her whole back. It was fucking terrifying. She called it the blood eagle."

"Do you know what a blood eagle is?"

"Not a clue. I figured it was some type of cartoon character or novel she had a fascination with."

"A blood eagle is an ancient Viking torture method used on their worst enemies. Kristy was blood eagled, Liz. She wasn't supposed to survive. The killer doesn't know she's alive. We haven't released any information on her situation."

"So, that bitch is the killer?"

John nodded. "And we have to find her before she kills again. Where is the club?"

"Long gone. They demolished the area years ago to build a cinema complex and restaurant in Hollywood. I really didn't know her that well. Her name was never spoken. She was only addressed as Mistress, and she had a pretty regular stable of customers who came to her for whippings and other forms of torture, which, as I stated, they paid her well for."

John sat back in his chair and looked at the others in the room. "I think we need to hold a press conference regarding Kristy Yates without telling the media what hospital she is in. We need to let them know she's alive."

Jim shook his head. "Bad move if you ask me. First, we need to talk to the kid. We need to know what she remembers about her attacker and see if she saw the person's face before we release details. Then, when we do release something, you can't leave this kid here. She will have to be hidden in a place where no one can get to her."

John nodded, and Sara asked, "Are we ready to bring Kristy out of the coma?"

Everyone nodded, and Sara began lowering the dosage of medication being administered to Kristy that had basically paralyzed her lungs. The ventilator remained in place until it was clear that Kristy could breathe on her own. She responded quickly to the withdrawal of drugs and began to cough on the breathing tube, and it was removed quickly.

Kristy shuddered a few times and coughed after the ventilator had been removed, and Liz asked Sara, "Is she okay?"

"Her throat is irritated as are her lungs and diaphragm. She will get more stable as I reduce the medications. I didn't use opioids. I used two shorter acting drugs, and since she has only been on the ventilator for about forty hours and is young, she will stabilize. Just relax."

Kristy began to moan and jerk. Her eyes sprang open, and she yelled with a raspy voice, "Leave me be. Who are you? Why are you doing this to me?" Her eyes were open, but she couldn't focus, and she just stared off at a wall as Sara continued to lower the medications. It took nearly an hour, but when the medications were out of her system, she began taking deep breaths with her eyes closed.

"It is going to take several hours for her to wake up. There's no reason to wait around. I will call you as soon as she is alert. It might be tonight or tomorrow."

Jim waved to John to walk out of the room. Chris and Sam followed the two men, and Jim walked them into an empty waiting room next door and shut the door. "John, you have to get that kid to the lair."

"Just how the hell am I supposed to do that?"

"I don't know, but once the killer knows that kid is alive, she will hunt out every hospital and sooner or later find her and that will be that."

"And her mother? How the hell do we explain it to her?"

"Her mother is in just as much danger as the kid. They both need to be taken to the lair."

Chris was leaning against the wall. "How are you going to get the kid and the mother to the lair without tipping off where they are going?"

Sam spoke up, "Sara owns the hospital, right?" All heads nodded. "Then why can't she have a private hospital for endangered patients that is underwritten by the Bureau?"

"Sam, you want me to tell Liz Yates that she and her daughter are being moved to a Bureau safehouse that has all of the medical equipment needed to treat her daughter and keep her safe?" John asked.

"Do you have any other ideas? Once we move her to your lair, we can draw out the killer by doing a press conference and then have someone pose as the kid in the hospital and give the killer an open invitation to try and kill her. She makes her move, and the Eagle takes her down."

"I don't know, Sam. We have to have a real body in that bed when we make the release. I have to convince Sara and Liz that we have a secure location run by the Bureau and attended to by Sara, and she can't know where she is. I can't put the kid in the operating rooms. I suppose the guest rooms would be okay, but we would need to move the girl and her mother under the cover of night and while they're sedated."

Sam smiled. "You can do all of those things, John. You've done it before."

CHAPTER TWELVE

"As in alive?"

"You look so peaceful hanging there, Trevor. One of my best angels yet."

Trevor was barely conscious. He had flailed when Joann put the saltwater on his back and lungs. "Why, Joann, why?"

"Oh, that's a complex question, Trevor. You're a lawyer, so talking to you is in many ways like speaking to a wall. I have such big plans for my life and for my love of blood eagles. I'm growing stronger and stronger with each kill, and the perfection keeps growing as I work. I have ten percent stock in Black Robotics. It was a gift from Steven years ago for services rendered. I can't have you fucking up the sale that is my retirement money."

"You are killing for the fun of it?"

"No. It's my art, a way of expressing myself by taking a dirty human animal and turning it into a majestic creature. You may not get wings when you die, but right now you have them. I can keep you alive for days with the right amount of pressure taken off your diaphragm and lungs."

"You're a monster."

"Oh, Trevor, that is just rude. You were once majestic, now you're revolting."

Joann pulled a scalpel off of a table in the cold room and ran the blade down Trevor's left lung. He screamed and then the lung opened and collapsed. "Ah, the pink flesh of the inside of your lung. At least that is beautiful. It will turn dark quickly as it has no oxygen."

Trevor began to thrash around on the hook. "Ah, you're suffocating, but you still have one good lung. You will no longer be able to speak, however, as every ounce of your energy must go into trying to breathe and stay alive. It's an involuntary thing, you see. Your brain needs the oxygen, and your autonomic nervous system won't let you stop breathing without a fight. Now, I'm not going to lie to you, if you think that you have been in pain so far, you haven't felt anything yet." She cut a piece off of Trevor's left lung and held it in front of his face then his nose. He opened his mouth for breath, and she shoved the flesh into his mouth and held his jaw shut. "Enjoy the flavor, Trevor. You have another involuntary situation here. Your brain needs air more than this flesh, so you are about to swallow it."

Joann released his jaw, and Trevor fought for air as the section of lung went down his throat. He was able to whisper, "Monster" as she held the scalpel to his face then moved behind him and stood on a step stool. She grabbed his right lung and pulled it with all her might. It dislodged from the airway, and Trevor shuddered for several minutes before he died.

"How rude. I was just trying to be a good host. Bailey Black came to see me today. She is next. She had the audacity to threaten me and thinks I had something to do with Steven's death." She grabbed Trevor's legs and pulled his body out of the cold room and into the robotics room. She picked up the remote and allowed the upper rail that held his body to move him along the line until he was over a large steel box. "Your brain still has some function, Trevor. I know that, so you can still hear me even though you're dead. I'm going to drop you into this custom-made unit. It's a grinder and incinerator. You will most likely feel the blades as you're ground to a pulp, but you won't feel the flames."

Joann pressed a button on the remote, and Trevor's body dropped into the unit. The lid closed, and the sound of the blades was muted by sound proofing. She could hear the cracking of bones and the shredding of flesh and then the flames ignited.

"How do you want to do this?" Chris asked John as Sara and Sam looked on.

"Release the security detail. Sara, we are going to need an ambulance. Is Kristy stable enough to move?"

"I will sedate her again, but she should be fine. I'm going to have to set up a set of dummy transfer documents for her medical file. You'll need to explain this to Liz. You're also going to have to explain why she will be under sedation in order to be taken to a Bureau safehouse."

"I can handle that. Do we have everything to care for the girl?"

"Yes. I will have to bring Karen in to help me monitor her; I may also need Cindy."

Jim was leaning against a wall when Sara said Cindy's name. "I don't want Cindy pulled into danger."

"She will be helping care for Kristy. There will be no danger. The danger is going to be for the person that is going to be in that room when John and Sam do the press conference and let the killer know Kristy is alive."

"I'm about her size and build. I'll do it." Sam said hesitantly.

"Are you sure, Sam? I will have to hook you up to an IV and monitor you because you have to look the part."

"Yeah, okay. It's the only way we are going to flush out this killer. Who will be my protection?"

Jim stepped forward. "I will be with you twenty-four seven if need be."

"I will be with you, too," said Chris. "I'm not going to let anything happen to you."

Sam looked at John and asked, "And what about the Eagle?"

"He will be there as well. The question is, are we dealing with just one killer or more than one? If the killer has help, we might get someone who works with her and is sent to kill Kristy outright. I doubt that this killer will try to take the girl again. The killer will also know that there will be protection on her, so unless the killer's invisible, she's going to have to work extra hard to get to her without being spotted and that will be some trick since we will secure the whole floor."

Chris looked around the ICU unit through the glass doors of the room they were in and said, "The ICU should be cleared of patients. Only Sam should be here. This gal may decide to take out more people or screw up and kill the wrong person. Sara, can you move these beds?"

"Yes. We have another setup on the other side of the building, so I can clear this whole section and lock it down."

Sam was standing near John and asked, "So, when do you want me in bed?" Jim chuckled, and she frowned. "I'm putting my life on the line, and you're laughing? You're an asshole."

"Hey, don't blame me. It sounded like you and John were going to have sex."

Sara laughed as did John. Sara said, "When this is all over, we just might have to give Sam's new home one hell of a housewarming party, if you know what I mean."

John and Sam blushed as Jim laughed. John said, "Sam, it won't be until tomorrow. It's late afternoon. We will hold a press conference in the morning, then you will come back here, and we will get you set up. Are you sure you want to do this?"

"Fuck no. Are you kidding me? Some psycho killer is blood eagling people, and I'm going to be the bait. I'm not sure about anything, but we have to protect Kristy, and we have to catch this killer. I don't see any other options, do you?"

John leaned down and kissed her on the cheek. "I won't let anything happen to you, Sam."

"You bet your sweet ass you won't."

Beverly was working on reports in her office when her cellphone rang, and the person on the other end of the line said, "Trevor is dead."

"Jesus Christ! What did you do, Joann?"

"I'm protecting my interests. I had a visit this morning from Bailey Black."

"So? She delivers your mail, right?"

"Yes, but this was not a friendly visit. She accused me of being involved with Steven's death and threatened me."

"That was pretty damn bold of her."

"I'm worried."

"You should be. You have exposed yourself too much this time. You are not killing undercover. You're killing in the open, and you have law enforcement and the Eagle after you."

"Yeah. It's the Eagle that I'm worried about."

"I have been telling you from the start that he's going to kill you."

"If the Eagle is a he, I'm fine."

"What the hell are you talking about? Of course the Eagle is a man. What would make you think otherwise?"

"I don't know. There was just something in Bailey's demeanor when she was in my office today. She told me that she knew I had something to do with Steven's death and if she found out I would die a thousand times more brutally than he did."

"Wow! She really said that to you?"

"Yes. I mean, she knows the club scene; she knows about Liz and Kristy, but she obviously doesn't know that Kristy is dead."

"That's where I really think you made your fatal mistake, Joann. If you had just killed her quietly as revenge, that would have been one thing, but to kill the girl and her father on the same night in the same room? And dumping the bodies the way you did. I think that will be the fatal flaw in your plan for the Eagle."

"If the Eagle's a man, I'll be fine. I'm concerned that perhaps the Eagle is a woman. I'm no lesbian, and if Bailey is the Eagle, then you're right, and I've overplayed my hand. Law enforcement must surely think that Steven and Kristy's killer is a man. They thought the killer was a man when I killed Lester. I feel like an idiot on the Kristy front. I should have just killed her and ground her up. I made a mistake there."

"Joann, you murdered a father and daughter on the same day! You don't think that Liz hasn't told law enforcement of the connection between the two by now?"

"Only if Liz knows about Steven's death."

"You blood eagled two people and left them in public. A blind person could connect those fuckin' dots. Now that you've killed Trevor, the only friend you have in the world is me."

"I still have three angels alive in my cooler, and I will create more after you sell the stock."

"I'm the only friend that you have, Joann. You might be well undercover at the moment, but Bailey knows your cruel streak, and if you move to kill her, I think you will get more than you bargained for."

"What do you mean?"

"If she is the Eagle, then you're in even more danger. She knows who you are, what you are, and what you're capable of doing. She might not know the depths of your depravity…"

"Creativity, Beverly, creativity. I transform ugly human animals into something beautiful. Most of my angels were just homeless vagabonds, hookers, and other urchins that society would never miss."

"You see it your way; I see it mine. I am going to try to put your stock up for sale in the next few days. If I were you, I would keep clear of Bailey. Leave your 'art' alone for a few weeks until this blows over. Only Steven and Kristy have seen your face when you killed them, right?"

"No. All of my victims see my beautiful face before I kill them, but Steven and Kristy are the only people I killed that I put out in public outside of Lester."

"Just keep a low profile. I'm not stripping to get you street meat again, and you aren't going to strip off your clothes and hunt for your prey yourself, are you?"

"No."

"Then just leave things be. I'm sure I'm going to get more visits from the cops and FBI. And now with Trevor missing, there will be a missing persons report out for him, but no one knows you two were together, right?"

"Right. Trevor came to my condo from the office. He didn't talk to anyone that I'm aware of."

"Leave a sleeping dog lie, Joann. As I said, I'm the only person who knows your secret, and I'm an accessory to murder in helping you get Steven and the others, so I'm not talking. Just leave things alone and we will speak again in a couple of days."

Beverly hung up the line, and Joann sat back on the couch in her living room, nude, and licked Trevor's blood from her fingers. "It's easier said than done, Beverly. I have the taste for it now. I want to try eating some of my angels, and the ones in the cooler have been there too long. I need a fresh canvas to sculpt and snack on."

Liz and Kristy were sleeping on gurneys in the ambulance when Jim pulled it into the lair's parking garage. John and Chris moved Kristy first and handed her off to Sara and Karen. Jim called out to Sara, "Is Cindy coming over?"

"Yes, Jim. I called her. Can you help get Liz out of the ambulance, please?"

Chris was pushing the gurney with Liz on it as John walked the hallway. Once she was in the room with Kristy, Chris looked at John and asked, "What did you tell Liz?"

"Follow my instructions or die."

"That's one way of getting someone's attention."

Sam had pulled into the structure at the lair. Jim saw her and asked, "Are you going to see Sandy tonight?"

"I haven't decided. I need rest."

Once the two women were settled in, John called the group into the conference room. "Okay, we are only going to get one shot at this. I called Trevor's office, and they have not heard a word from him today. The building surveillance cameras show nothing out of the ordinary. When he left the building, it was late, and he left alone, which is his M.O. I agree that Mr. Craig if not already dead will be soon. I have scheduled a press conference for nine tomorrow morning. I let the media know this is with regard to Kristy Yates in the hopes that it will get the killer's attention. Sam, you have the night to do what you please. Meet me at my office at eight a.m., and we will go over the press conference and then move from there. It's going to be a long few days, so I suggest that everyone go home and get some rest."

Jim asked, "What are you going to do?"

"I'm going to work with Sara and Karen to bring Kristy out of her coma and to see if there is any information that she can give on her attacker."

"What about your sketch artist?"

"I can't get anyone in the Bureau involved. I have photos of everyone we suspect in this case. I'm going to show her mug shots and see if she sees the person who hurt her."

"You have photos of potential suspects, John, but not of all the possible killers. If she doesn't see her attacker, that doesn't mean shit. You need to add others that are involved in her life. You need photos of her teachers and close friends at school. She has some shit with the library, right?" John nodded. "Then you need to get photos of the people that are involved there as well. Fuck. Get photos of that librarian and her staff."

"Now, you're really reaching, Jim."

"That's our fuckin' job, John. I'm sure there is nothing there, but the more ground that we cover, the faster we will know who we are dealing with."

Jim paused, and Chris asked, "And if we show her all of this and there is nothing?"

Jim pulled a cigarette out of his top left pocket, lit it, snapped his Zippo shut, and said, "If we go through all of this and she sees no one, then we're all fucked, and Sam isn't getting into that hospital bed."

"Look," John said, "it's our job to put our lives on the line to protect the public. This killer defies logic. She's been off the radar for over a decade then suddenly turned up with two very public killings, and in the end, it is a father and daughter. It has been less than two days, and all is quiet, though Trevor Craig is now missing and presumed dead. I agree with you. Sara needs to wake the Yates girl, and we need photos of anyone she would have interacted with in her circle. I also agree that if she offers no leads, Sam shouldn't get in that bed. In fact, I don't think we should put Sam in the bed at all."

All eyes were upon John. Jim lifted his head up as smoke billowed from his lungs.

"What the fuck are you talking about?"

"We'll use a lifelike AI doll instead."

"Like a mannequin?"

"Sort of. The Bureau uses dolls for training. They are, for all intents and purposes, human. They can simulate breathing, a pulse, can be warmed to regular body temperature, are anatomically correct, and can even bleed."

"Where the hell do you get dolls like that?" Sara asked.

"We have several manufacturers who deliver them to us. We can't shoot, stab, and injure real people, so we use them for training. I can get

Sandy the specifications I need with information from Kristy, and she can build a doll that looks just like her."

Karen had been listening without commenting as Sara grilled John. "So, can you have sex with these dolls?"

"Yes."

"Can the general public buy them?"

"No. These are custom built for the military and other government agencies. However, there is a huge market in AI sex dolls, and the public does purchase those."

"I'm sorry, John, but you're creeping me out."

Karen spoke up, "What John is talking about is real. I am very familiar with them. We used them in medical school. It gave us the opportunity to perform medical procedures on near living people without the risk of killing someone. However, there is an inherent danger in AI that many computer scientists and others have warned about, and that is the danger of AI becoming self-aware."

Jim started laughing. "So, you're saying that these dolls could start to think on their own?"

"Yes. Not just dolls but computer systems as a whole. We walk a tight rope every day with this type of technology. The world has become more and more dependent upon these types of systems. Most of the nation's and the world's infrastructure is operated by computers. If you think that humans hacking computer systems or stealing data is scary, imagine a computer system becoming self-aware."

"As in alive?"

"Yes."

Jim laughed and put out his cigarette. "I'm sorry, but you have watched a few too many science fiction movies. This shit isn't a real threat."

John chimed in, "Look, this is not the time to get into the dangers of AI. Karen, please get all of Kristy's measurements for me. You and Sara get those right down to her eye color, hair color, and skin tone. I will then get Sandy working on the doll right away. We should be able to have it by morning, and we will use it instead of putting Sam's life on the line."

"For fuck's sake, John, if you have this technology, why the hell have we been putting our lives on the line so many times?" Jim asked.

"Jim, these aren't walking talking robots. They are controlled by computers. This is the perfect situation to use them in. They are no substitute if you need a human who can move and think in real time. A teenager on her death bed is believable. If we had to have her moving about, we would need Sam, or you, me, or anyone else."

Sara and Karen left the room, and Cindy asked, "Are you going to train it?"

"There is no reason for that. We will set it up on life support and monitor the room."

Jim asked, "Who is going to monitor it?"

"That depends on what we learn from the Yates girl."

CHAPTER THIRTEEN

*"This is a game, and
I'm not going to fall for it."*

Beverly had the radio on in her car as she drove home. The news about Kristy Yates' survival was to be explained in more detail in the morning, but Beverly wasted no time calling Joann.

"Kristy Yates is alive."

"WHAT?"

"She's alive. There will be a joint press conference with the FBI and the Sheriff's Department tomorrow."

"That's not possible. There must be some mistake."

"Was she breathing when you left her, Joann?"

"Yes, but I anchored her through her lungs to the ceiling on her knees. There's no way she would have been able to breathe more than a few minutes after I left her. The pressure of her body release onto her frame would suffocate her."

"Well, I just heard on the radio that she's alive."

Joann had the phone to her ear, and her eyes were bulging as she stared at the ceiling of her office. "There is no way she's alive. If she were and she could speak, they would have gotten to me by now. This is some type of trap."

"Joann, if the damn kid hasn't spoken, they might not know who her attempted killer was, but if she is able to talk, you're fucked."

"Someone is screwing with me. Someone wants me to believe she's alive, so they can flush me out into the open. I'm sure they'll say which hospital she's at, if she really is alive, and they'll set a trap to see if I'll show up."

"You overplayed your hand, Joann. They are going to find you. I believe that the kid is still alive. I think you fucked up. I think that your zeal for punishing Liz clouded your judgment and that you missed something and somehow Kristy survived."

"You don't know what you're talking about. You have no idea what a blood eagle does to the body. Sure, people can live for a day or up to a week but to put someone back together after I have done my work? Not possible. You have no idea what it would take. It's impossible to reverse. I'm telling you she couldn't survive."

"Then why would the FBI and Sheriff say she did?"

"To flush me out. Even if the kid had somehow survived, she wouldn't be able to speak or even be conscious. She would have to be in a coma, and there is no information that they can get from a comatose patient. No. This is a game, and I'm not falling for it."

"My ass is on the line here, too, Joann. I helped you get victims; I got you Steven. If they get to you, they will get to me, and I'm not going to die protecting you."

"You need to calm down, Beverly. The kid is dead. This is some last-ditch effort to get me to come into the light. The kid's dead; her father is dead, and I need to take out her mother."

"Don't even think about it. No more killing, Joann. I'm certain, alive or dead, the kid's mother has told police about the relationship between Steven and the kid and that he is her father. Liz can't connect you, but she sure as hell could tie me and others to your old dungeon. You wore your fuckin' latex masks, but you forget there is another way to identify you."

"My tattoo?"

"I doubt there are many women with your body and build with a blood eagle tattoo covering the whole of their back. That is the one way you can be identified."

"Like the police are going to grab me and strip me. Only a few people know about the tattoo, and none of them are people that I work with or people who use the library. For the most part, everyone who has even seen my tattoo is dead."

"Bailey Black knows about it. She may not know you, but she knows the tattoo."

"So? She doesn't know it's me. She's no threat."

"Unless she's the Eagle. If she puts two and two together, she will come for you or go to the cops and try and identify you as a suspect."

"No one suspects me right now. Yates is dead, and I'm not going to stick my head out of my hole to allow anyone in."

"Well, I'll be watching the news conference in the morning, and I suggest you do the same."

Sandy received John's request for the doll and sent the information over to the tech department. Sam called her right after John had, and Sandy said, "Sounds like you've been having an interesting day."

"Interesting, disturbing, nauseating. The list pretty much goes on."

"What's up?"

"I wanted to see if you were available for dinner?"

"Sure. I requested the doll for John, but it won't be ready until morning. I have most of my reports finished, so I will leave around seven. Where would you like to eat? As if I need to ask."

Sam laughed. "You know where. After that, I was thinking we could go over to my new home. It's ready, and I thought I could take you on a tour."

"Sure! You have a multimillion dollar mansion in Malibu. I definitely want to see the finished product."

"Then I will see you at Santiago's. Seven thirty?"

"I'll be there, gorgeous." Sandy hung up the line and smiled to herself. "She is falling for me. I knew she would."

Bailey had just finished her route and was getting ready to go home when she heard the radio report on the attempted murder of Kristy Yates. She sat in her truck looking up at the post office as tears filled her eyes, and she slammed her hands down on the steering wheel. "She killed my brother and tried to kill his daughter. The bitch must die."

Jim, John, and Chris had been working with Liz for several hours to find photos of people affiliated with Kristy. Kristy had been groggy but now was alert, and the four sat in the living room of the guest quarters of the lair putting the finishing touches on the screenshots for John's tablet when Sara walked in and announced that Kristy was awake.

"Can she speak?" John asked.

"Not well. She's off the ventilator and slightly sedated. She is in a lot of pain, but it won't cloud her judgment."

Liz stood up and said, "I want to see her."

Sara walked the group back to the bedroom where Kristy was partially sitting up and smiling as Liz entered the room. Liz sat down on the edge of the bed and kissed Kristy's face and told her how much she loved her. The young girl was grinning from ear to ear, although the pain she was feeling was evident. She looked at the others in the room and whispered, "Where am I?"

John responded, "You are in protective custody along with your mother, Kristy. I'm sure you are sore."

"I feel like someone ran over me with a tractor. What happened?"

"You don't remember?"

"It all seems like a nightmare. This still feels like I'm in a nightmare."

John nodded. "It wasn't a nightmare, Ms. Yates. You are alive because of the heroic efforts of a lot of people. However, the person who did this to you is still out there, and I need to find him."

Kristy looked at her mother and asked, "Are you okay, Mom?"

"I am now. I know you're hurting, but this is FBI Deputy Director John Swenson. The other man is FBI Agent Chris Mantel. The pretty young woman standing next to him is Sheriff Samantha Pritchard, and the rumpled old man at the foot of your bed is …"

Kristy coughed a little, interrupting her mother, and said, "That's Sheriff Jim O'Brian."

Liz nodded. "Do you two know each other?"

"He spoke at my school a few times. He doesn't hold back. Sheriff Pritchard, what are you doing here?"

"Watching over you. Try and keep your conversation to a minimum. You will need your strength. We need your help."

"Yes, ma'am. You're one of my idols."

Sam smiled as John pulled a stool up next to the bed with his tablet in hand. "Kristy, can you tell me the last thing you remember before waking up here?"

"I went to bed last night. I think it was last night. At some point my mom woke me in the early morning to tell me she was going to work. I remember falling back to sleep and then the nightmare began."

"Tell me about the nightmare."

"Someone came into my bedroom and put some stuff up my nose, and I couldn't move. They picked me up and carried me out of my room and threw me in the trunk of a car. I was out for a bit and then woke up naked on a table while a woman in a mask talked."

"What did she say?"

"She was talking to someone else. She was telling him how flattered she had been by his compliments and that she felt bad that she had to do something to him."

"Did she say a name?"

"I don't recall, but I heard a machine start up and then the man screamed and got quiet."

"Did you ever see the man?"

"I don't think so. I heard the woman say what a wonderful angel he was and then I started to pray."

"You prayed?"

"I did, but it didn't help. She started hurting me. She tore into my back, and it got hard to breath, and the pain kept getting worse, and she kept injecting me with medicine that woke me up. I was on a machine, and it was cutting pieces of me off, and she was feeding them to animals and talking to me."

"Do you remember what she said?"

"She said that I had nice breasts for my age and that she was peeling them away. She said I was going to be an angel and that my mom should have never gotten between her and what she wanted and that this was punishment for her."

"Did you see the person's face?"

"Once. The machine hung me on some kind of rack, and I remember I was crying out, but the woman wouldn't help me. She had been wearing a strange red mask but pulled it off and told me to look into her beautiful face."

"Did you know her?"

"Yes, but now I can't remember who she was."

"I have some photographs I would like you to look at. Can you do that?" Kristy nodded. "I want you to look at these carefully and tell me if you see her." John put his tablet up in front of Kristy, and she used a weak right hand to slowly flip the pages on the tablet and looked at each set of pictures carefully as everyone in the room looked on. She paused after the third swipe and stared at the screen. "What do you see, Kristy?"

"I know this woman."

Kristy had her finger on a photo, and John looked at Bailey Black's picture on the screen. "Is that the woman who hurt you?"

"No, but I know her. I have met her before."

"But she didn't hurt you?"

"No." Kristy slowly flipped through the pages then paused again and stared. She winced a little as she tried to move in her bed then pointed at a photo and said, "This woman … I have dealt with her several times."

John looked at the photo of Beverly Hampton. "You dealt with her? What do you mean?"

"She was a volunteer with several programs I was involved in. She makes donations to my school as well as other projects. She is involved with the library as well, but I don't know what she does." She looked through the photos and stopped, and tears welled up in her eyes. She put her finger on a photo and said, "I saw him."

John looked at the photo. It was Steven Black. "Where did you see him?"

"In a cold room after he had been hurt by the woman. He and I were hanging next to each other."

"Did he speak to you?"

"No. The woman just kept calling him a beautiful angel and saying how she had transformed him. She said the same to me, but I remember the look of horror on his face and the sadness. She kept hurting him with a stick." She thumbed across the screens and stopped, her eyes wide open. "I know her. I know her!" Kristy's fingers and hands began to shake, and John looked at the photo. It was Joann Fontaine."

"Is this the person who hurt you?"

"I know her. She's the librarian downtown. She worked with a lot of kids in programs through the library."

The photo was a profile shot and not a head shot.

"Have you ever seen this woman outside the library?"

"Yes, I have."

"Do you know where?"

"No, but several of these people were in my nightmare." She paused then looked at John and said, "A tattoo."

"A tattoo?"

"A horrible, hideous tattoo. The woman who hurt me showed me a tattoo on her back. It was like an angel but not an angel. She said that I had been transformed to look like it."

"How did she show you this tattoo?"

"She was wearing a white coat, and she walked away from me as I hung on some kind of hook, and she removed the coat and was naked. She raised her arms into the air and said, 'Behold your transformation.' I didn't understand. I was in agony, but the image covered her whole back from just above her butt to her neck and was bloody and gross looking."

"I don't know if you can answer this, but was it ink or real blood on her back?"

"It wasn't running. It looked like an open wound or was created to look like one, but I think it was just ink."

"Is there anything else you remember about this woman?"

Kristy took a deep breath and closed her eyes. Sara pulled on John's arm and said, "She needs to rest, John."

"I need to know more about this woman. Give her a stimulant."

"I can't. It's too risky for her heart right now. Let her sleep. We can try again later."

"I need to know if this is the person who did this to her."

"Don't you think she would have started screaming or had some other violent reaction if she recognized this woman as her attacker?"

John nodded. "Perhaps, but she is also in shock, so her reactions can't be trusted completely."

"What does that say about everyone she has pointed out? You have people that you should be talking to if not investigating. Let her rest, John. She has to rest."

The group stepped out of the room, and Jim took a cigarette out of his top left pocket and walked out of the operating area and to the deck off the lair's foyer and lit the smoke. The rest followed him and after taking a few big hits off the cigarette with his back to the others he said, "Find the tattoo, and you'll find the killer. You can put that doll or AI or whatever the fuck that thing is into the hospital bed, but this killer is way too sophisticated to try and get to the kid like that. She is going to count on Yates not remembering due to the agony of what she did to her. We need to start looking for that tattoo."

John and Chris were sitting on lounge chairs, and Sam was standing near the entrance to the lair holding herself against the cold sea air. "And just how the fuck are we going to get to see that tattoo? Are you going to go up to the women the kid pointed at and ask, 'Oh, by the way, will you strip off your top and turn around? I want to see your back.'"

Chris laughed at Sam's response in spite of himself, and John asked Jim, "Do you think it would be worthwhile to go see Bailey Black again?"

"You think she's the killer?"

"She was the most candid person we've spoken to, but I don't think she's the killer. I think if we see her and ask her to show us her back, she will. And if she does, and it's blank, I have a pretty good idea who our killer is."

Chris and Sam stared at John as Jim turned around. "You think you know who the killer is?" Jim asked. John nodded. "And you think that Ms. Black will lead you to this killer?"

"Yes."

No one said a word for several minutes, then Sam asked, "What makes you think that Ms. Black will cooperate?"

"She told us about the tattoo that Kristy just spoke about. If she's the killer, she will run and hide or refuse to show us her back, but I think she'll strip off her clothes and show us her back without a thought."

Jim threw his cigarette off the edge of the deck into the sea. "Then let's go see Ms. Black."

"Do you want me to go with you?" Chris asked.

"No. I want you to go see Ms. Hampton."

"Do you want me to ask her to strip off her clothes?"

"I want you to prod her about Joann Fontaine and press her on the Black murder."

"What is that going to accomplish?"

"Ms. Hampton is involved in these killings. I don't know how yet, but I feel she not only knows who the killer is, but she is assisting and has assisted her. She might even be the killer."

Sam unfolded her arms and asked Jim for a cigarette. He lit it for her and handed it to her. "So, if Black is cleared and Hampton is assisting the killer or is the killer, where does that leave Joann Fontaine?" she asked.

"She is an enigma. I doubt she's truly celibate. I think one of those women is the killer, and the other is the enabler."

"Then why not come at Fontaine head-on?"

"If you have to ask that question, you're right about getting out of police work."

Jim shook his head as he walked to the foyer. "Let's go see Ms. Black at her apartment, John. Sam, you take the night off. It's six thirty. Keep your phone close and just stay away from people tonight."

CHAPTER FOURTEEN

"Damn, Jim! What did you find?"

Sandy was sitting at a table in Santiago's when she saw Sam walk in. She waved to her, and Sam walked over to the table and sat down. "I need a stiff drink, Javier. Can I get a triple Jack and a beer back, please?"

Sandy was looking at Sam's white face and asked, "What happened?"

"I fucked up. I fucked up, and someone could die."

"What do you mean?"

"John thinks he knows who killed Black and tried to kill Yates, and I just walked right into a buzz saw."

Javier brought the drinks over to the table, and Sam shot the booze then drank some beer and asked for another. Sandy looked at her and said, "Six ounces of alcohol on an empty stomach is not a good plan, Sam. Let's get some food."

Sam nodded and when Javier came back to the table with the second round of drinks the two ordered, and Sam lifted the shot in the air to Sandy and said, "A toast!"

"What are we toasting?"

"My impending death."

John and Jim arrived at Bailey's apartment at eight p.m. The two men walked up to the front door, but before they could knock it opened, and Bailey stood in the entry in a robe with wet hair. "I was wondering when you two would be back. Come in."

John and Jim entered. "So, you have been expecting us?" John asked.

"Of course. You don't have a conversation like the one that we had and not come back to the sister of the victim, and I'm pretty sure I know why you're here."

"And why are we here?"

Bailey didn't respond but walked into a brightly lit eating area of her kitchen, turned her back to the two men, and dropped her robe. Jim looked at her nude body as did John, and then after several seconds Bailey asked, "Did you get the answer you came for?"

"How did you know?" John asked.

"Because there is a bitch out there who killed my brother and tried to kill my half-sister, and I just figured out who she is, or I'm pretty fuckin' sure who she is. I heard on the news that Kristy is alive."

"She is," John responded.

"Is she safe? Because that bitch will go after her if she learns where she is."

"I don't think she will, Ms. Black. Please put your robe back on. Who is the person you suspect of being the killer?"

Bailey laughed. "Oh no, Director Swenson. I'm not telling you that. Oh no. She's mine. She killed my father and my brother, and she tried to kill my sister. She will be coming for me tonight, I expect, but I have a surprise for her. I know she's coming."

John sat down on one of the small dining room chairs as Jim stood. "Look, Ms. Black, I understand your desire for revenge, but you can't take the law into your own hands."

"Why not? The Iron Eagle does, and you haven't caught him. That's who she wants. She wants the Iron Eagle. I know that now. I'm not going to let that bitch get in bed with him literally and figuratively to create the perfect killing couple."

Jim spoke up, "That's not how the Iron Eagle works, Ms. Black. He wants to get to the killer as badly as you do, and believe me, no magical couple is going to come from his finding her."

"And just how the fuck do you know that, Sheriff?"

"Because I know the identity of the Iron Eagle. Because I have worked side by side with him for two decades. I know him, and I know his wife, who is his soulmate. We have heard all of the rumors, Ms. Black, but I can tell you that the only thing that is going to happen to the killer is something bad."

Bailey turned around quickly and looked Jim up and down. "You're full of shit. You're a cop. You can't know who the Eagle is and let him keep killing."

"I know who he is, and I want him to keep killing."

Bailey put her robe on and sat down at the table. Jim followed. She looked at John and asked, "Do you know who the Eagle is?"

"I do."

Bailey laughed hard. Her robe was wide open in the front, and Jim was staring at her breasts. "The FBI and Sheriff's Department know who the Eagle is? That's rich, and you wonder why people don't trust the cops. So, the Eagle wants to get to this killer before she kills again?"

"Yes."

"I see, and is the Eagle nearby?"

"Yes."

"So, is he like Batman? You shine a light in the sky or call him on some red phone, and he comes running?" Bailey was laughing as she spoke.

John was stone-faced, "No. He's usually ahead of us in these types of cases, and we know he is hunting."

"Oh, I see. You two want to catch the Eagle in action. Is that it? I tell you who I'm after and then you tell the Eagle, and you get to the scene before him and catch him in the act of killing?" Jim took out a cigarette and asked if he could smoke. Bailey said, "Sure. Hand me one of those fuckin' things. I gave up the habit years ago, but once in a while they taste good." Jim lit it and handed it to her. She took a couple of deep drags off the cigarette and leaned back in her chair, her robe now wide open. "I see you admiring my body, Sheriff O'Brian. Do you want to fuck me?"

Jim had smoke rising from his cigarette that forced his right eye shut. "You are beautiful, but no I would not."

"Why the fuck not? Are you too good for me? Are you too good to fuck a hot, willing woman?"

"I'm in a relationship, so I'll admire the view while you tell us who you want to kill."

"There are only two people close to me that I would want to go after. One is painfully obvious and the other I doubt you even suspect."

John spoke up, "You mean Joann Fontaine?"

Bailey laughed and blew smoke in the air. "Impressive, Mr. Swenson, very impressive."

"Which one is the one that you are going after?" John asked.

"Beverly first. She is the easiest of the targets. Joann is a thousand times more savage and very, very dangerous. You see, you never see her coming. She's a secret who moves in darkness. She is the last one anyone would suspect of evil, but I know she is the personification of evil."

"And how do you know this?"

"To be honest, I didn't until a few hours ago when I heard that Kristy was still alive. She fucked up. I know Kristy was not supposed to be alive, and I don't know any of the details on how she survived being blood eagled, but once I heard the news, the pieces fell into place. All of those clubs, the scenes that were played out, the tattoo. I knew when I saw your car pull up that that's what you were here to see. You thought I was the killer. Tell me I'm wrong."

John was still as he responded, "I didn't think you were the killer, but, yes, we came here to ask to see your back. Now, if Ms. Fontaine is the killer, she would have the tattoo on her back."

"That's true, but I have never seen Joann nude, or at least I can't prove I have."

"What about Ms. Hampton? Have you seen her nude?" John asked.

"Parts of her. She has great tits, but she was laying on her back on a torture bondage cross all of the times that I saw her nude."

"Did the person torturing her have the tattoo because that would resolve the issue through the process of elimination?"

"Steven did her on the board as well as Liz Yates. Liz and Beverly were bottoms. I never saw either of them beat by the woman with the blood eagle tattoo."

"I don't understand. How can you be so sure she's the killer?"

Jim laughed at John's question. "Bailey isn't sure that Ms. Fontaine is the killer, are you Bailey? You have other reasons for wanting her dead. Even if she isn't the killer, you are going after her for other personal reasons, right?"

Bailey pulled her robe closed and stubbed out the cigarette. "She may not have killed my brother, but she is responsible for his death."

John's voice was angry, "Ms. Black, do you know that Joann Fontaine is a killer?"

"She is responsible for my brother's death and for the attempt on Kristy Yates' life."

"How do you know this?"

"Because she is an evil bitch. She is a user who manipulated my brother and father, who got in between me and my brother as well as between him and Liz after he knocked Liz up, and now she is looking to get people out of the way—me being next."

"Out of the way of what?"

"The missing stock. I'm sure you know by now about the missing stock."

John nodded. "There is now a missing trust attorney who handled the Black trust."

Bailey lowered her head. "She got to Trevor?"

"We don't have a body, but I feel strongly as does Sheriff O'Brian that that is the case."

"So, they are stalling your investigation, so that the stock can be sold, and she can disappear."

"Ms. Black, you're telling us that the killer is either Beverly Hampton or Joann Fontaine. You feel Fontaine is more dangerous than Hampton, but you have no proof that either one is a killer."

"I'm not the killer, Mr. Swenson. I have proven that to you, so yeah, it's one of those two, but no matter how you cut it Joann is the worst of the two, and I need to get her before the Eagle does."

Joann was eating dinner when the front desk called her penthouse. She listened for a few seconds and said, "Let her up." She hung up the line and sat back down at the table. She heard the elevator doors open and heard one of her slaves speaking in the distance. She took a sip of wine as the young woman entered the room with Joann's guest. The slave was then excused.

"Please have a seat. Do you mind if I finish my meal?" Sam sat down as Joann finished eating. "Would you like a glass of wine?"

"No, thank you. I have had a few drinks already this evening."

"I see. Rough day?"

"They are all rough in my line of work, Ms. Fontaine."

"I imagine they are. I don't envy your vocation, Sheriff. It is a thankless and dangerous job. I am a huge supporter of our law enforcement."

"I'm sure that you are. I know the library has put on all types of police awareness and appreciation programs."

"They are done under the guise of the library, but I am the one who puts them together."

Joann finished her meal then invited Sam to join her in the drawing room of the penthouse. Sam walked the room and looked out the wall length windows that looked down over the city. "This is one hell of a view you have from up here. Oriental décor. Impressive. Much like the foyer coming into your home, I didn't know that the library business paid so well."

Joann laughed as she sat down on a small sofa with her wine. "It doesn't. My family is very wealthy, and this was a present when I finished grad school. I picked it because of its proximity to the library and other downtown venues, so I wouldn't need a car. I'm impressed with your knowledge of decorating. Each of the rooms in my home are themed based on eras and cultures that I love. I love Japanese art and sculpture. It's sleek in its look and neat in appearance. The Japanese are a very neat and well-organized people with a fascinating history and culture."

"I see."

"So, what brings you to my home at nine thirty at night?"

"Steven Black."

"Poor Steven. I really liked him. What a cruel way to die."

"Indeed."

"What do you want to know about him?"

"Why you killed him."

"I beg your pardon?"

"I want to know why you killed Steven Black and attempted to kill Kristy Yates. And while I'm asking, do you know where attorney Trevor Craig is?"

Joann responded abruptly, "Sheriff, are you drunk?"

"Yes, but that's beside the point. Why, Ms. Fontaine?"

"I have never hurt anyone nor would I. I think that you should go home and sleep it off, Sheriff Pritchard. This is your career you're putting on the line."

"My career, indeed, if I were wrong, but I'm not, Ms. Fontaine. The question for me is how to deal with you."

"I don't understand."

"Well, I'm pretty sure that the Eagle knows you're the killer, and I'm also sure that he is in the area or will be shortly. I have heard about your fascination with him and your fantasy about him."

Joann smiled. "So, the Eagle is a man?"

"He is, indeed, and what a man he is, but things aren't going to work out the way you have imagined they would."

"Do you know him?"

"I know him very, very well." Joann moved to stand, but Sam pulled her gun and told her to sit.

"Sheriff, have you lost your mind?"

"Hardly. You are the one who is out of your mind."

Joann was wearing a red velvet robe, and Sam ordered her to stand and face the windows. Joann did as instructed, and Sam said, "Remove your robe, please."

"I'm sorry. I know you're gay, but I'm not."

"Remove the goddamned robe!"

"And if I don't?"

"I will shoot you in the back of the head and remove it myself."

John's cellphone rang, and he answered and heard Sandy's frantic voice on the other end of the line. "John, John. Jesus Christ! You have to save Sam!"

"What are you talking about Sandy?" Jim and Bailey were staring at him as he spoke.

"Sam liquored up on about nine ounces of Jack Daniels and two beers here at Santiago's, then we toasted, and she said she was going to die. She kissed me deeply and said she was off to see the blood eagle. I don't know what the fuck she was talking about, but I'm scared to death."

"She didn't tell you where she was going or who she was going to see?"

"No. She just told me she was going downtown near her offices and that she loved me."

"Okay, I have a pretty good idea where she is going." John hung up the line and asked Bailey, "Ms. Fontaine lives in a penthouse condo downtown, correct?"

"Yes. Two blocks from the library at 515 South Flower Street. Why?"

"Have you been to her home before?"

"Yes. It's on the fifty second floor, and she owns the whole floor. Why are you asking?"

"How do you access the unit?"

"Um … there are two private express elevators that open into the suite. One is the main elevator, and the other is a freight elevator that opens in the kitchen. What's going on?"

"That call was letting me know that the Eagle is on the move and that he is going to try and get Ms. Fontaine." Bailey smiled and sat back in her chair, allowing her robe to open freely once again.

Jim stood up and asked, "Aren't you concerned?"

"Not at all. If the Eagle is going to Joann's, then we know who the killer is. I just need to wait for the news story saying that Joann has disappeared, and I will know who has her." She sat up quickly. "You two aren't going to try and stop him, are you?"

John spoke, "We know who he is, but it is our job to try and at least look like we are trying to stop him."

She sat back in her chair, and Jim said, "This conversation never took place, Ms. Black."

"Nope. If the Eagle gets Joann, I will get the ten percent stock she stole, and I will be set for life, and it gets around my father's will. You're not going to share that secret, are you?"

John shook his head. "No, we will not. In fact, we don't want to know how you are going to get the stock so long as you aren't going to hurt anyone."

"Don't have to. If Joann goes missing, the stock will revert to me as it was given to me by my brother, who was manipulated into giving it to her many, many years ago. It's in the trust. The stock is mine as Steven never amended the will. It was just blinded in transfer, so my father didn't know who was getting it. Now go. Fast. But please don't stop the Eagle."

John and Jim rushed out of the apartment, and John got in the back of his truck as Jim drove.

"So, what now?" Jim asked as he watched John slipping into his body armor.

"Find the building and then the freight delivery area. I can find the express elevator to the penthouse. You ride up with me then hide while I get to Sam and Fontaine."

"What about Beverly Hampton?"

"Let's get the killer first; Hampton isn't going anywhere." Jim sped through the streets of downtown Los Angeles turning loudly onto Flower Street, tires squealing. "Do you want the locals on us, Jim? Easy, easy."

"Hey, Sam went on a suicide mission. What the fuck was she thinking?" The building came into view, and Jim followed the signs until he found the freight entrance, but it was blocked by piston guarded barricades. "John there's a damn key swipe card reader to lower the barricades."

John dug around in one of his duffle bags until he found a card reader. He ran the card through it, and it scanned millions of codes in a matter of seconds until it found the right one, and the barricades lowered, allowing them access. Jim pulled the truck in and then backed it up.

"Damn, Jim. What did you find?"

"A sign that says private elevator penthouse deliveries only."

"Well, they put out a welcome mat for us."

John put on the Eagle's mask, and Jim shuddered. "That thing still creeps me out."

"Yeah, well, let's move."

Once they were inside the elevator, Jim pressed the button and asked, "So, what are we hoping for?"

"Sam to still be alive and Joann Fontaine to have that tattoo."

Joann stood nude with her back to Sam. The tattoo of the blood eagle flowed across her back. Sam laughed. "I have to tell you, Ms. Fontaine, that is one ugly ass tattoo."

"So, what now, Sheriff? Are you going to cuff me and take me to jail?"

"No, no, no. You would be out tonight on bond. A tattoo isn't enough to hold you on. No," Sam said, swaying with the gun in her hand. "I think we have to come to a different arrangement."

"And what type of arrangement would that be?"

"An end to your terror."

The room was well lit, and Joann was standing in the center of the room against the wall of windows. What Sam couldn't see was what was in front of Joann, which was a Japanese katana sword in a mount on a table by the window in front of her. Joann stretched her arms up in the air, and the tattoo on her back seemed to come alive, and as she lowered her hands, she grabbed the sword and held it in front of her.

"So, Sheriff, you don't like the artwork on my back? You have no taste. It is a rendering of an ancient Viking torture method."

"I know what it is, Ms. Fontaine. Do you know the mythology behind that image?"

"I know a great deal, Sheriff. May I put my robe back on as I am getting a chill, or are we going to stand like this all night?"

The elevator opened into a well lit kitchen area where a young woman had her back to the two men as she was cleaning up dishes. Jim grabbed her from behind and covered her mouth.

"Where is Ms. Fontaine?" The girl pointed to a darkened hall, and Jim asked, "Is there anyone else here?" The girl nodded as Jim tranquilized her and left her in a corner of the kitchen.

The Eagle pointed to the corridor. "You first."

Jim nodded and made his way to the darkness and then faded into it. He could hear voices down a long hall, and he recognized Sam's voice and slurred speech. He followed the sound with the Eagle on his tail until he reached the room where the two women were. He looked around the corner and saw Joann's nude tattooed body facing the window and Sam with her gun trained on the woman. He pulled a tranquilizer gun from its holster and entered the room. "Sam!" Both Sam and Joann jumped. Jim had the gun trained on Joann who spun fast with the sword in her hands stretching out her arms in Sam's direction, the tip of the blade catching Sam near her head as Jim pulled the trigger striking her.

Jim rushed into the room as Sam began to sink to the floor. The Eagle made his way in as well and checked on Joann, who was out, and then got over to Sam, who was laying on the floor in a pool of blood as Jim tried to stop the bleeding from her neck.

"I found her, Jim."

Jim had tears in his eyes as he held Sam close and tried to stop the bleeding. "Yes, Sam. Yes, you did."

"She threw something at me. What was it?"

"I'm not sure, Sam."

"It's getting cold in here, Jim. What's going on?"

The Eagle had made his way to the two of them and saw the blood and then the sword on the ground near Joann's body. The Eagle removed his mask and looked into Sam's dying eyes. "Why Sam? Why did you do this?"

"You were right, John. The woman with the tattoo is the killer, and I found her. I'm getting so cold. Why am I getting so cold?"

Jim leaned down and kissed her face, "You're bleeding out, Sam. She caught you in the neck with some type of sword." John was kneeling next to the two of them as Sam began to lose consciousness.

"I'm dying, aren't I Jim?"

Jim started crying as he held her close. "Yes, Sam. I'm trying, but I can't stop the bleeding."

"Maria? Is that you?" Sam had a cold stare and a smile on her face as she spoke. "You're here, but you're dead." She was quiet as if listening to someone and then said, "Well, okay, that sounds like fun. Let's go." As her eyes began to close, neither man said a word.

Jim released her, and let her body lay on the floor. "She's gone. What the fuck happened?"

John got up and walked over to Joann, who was asleep on the floor, and picked up the sword. "Sam must not have spotted this in front of Fontaine. It's a katana, a Japanese fighting sword. She must have caught her throat with the end of the blade. Sandy told me on the phone that Sam had about nine ounces of alcohol at Santiago's tonight then toasted her own death and left to come here."

"Son of a bitch, John, son of a bitch." He cried without holding back, and John had tears in his eyes as well.

"She died a hero, Jim. She caught our killer. If she had been sober, she would have seen the sword."

"Jesus, John. She was just a kid. I tried to train her. I tried to protect her."

"You did the very best that you could, Jim. We all make mistakes."

"I just built her a new home. She was getting ready to start a new life."

John held Jim by the shoulders as he shuddered and wept. "I know, Jim, I know. There are no words for this type of loss, and you know that. Take her body down to the truck and wrap her in one of the blankets I have in the back."

"What are you going to do?"

"I have to clear this unit and see what we are dealing with. I will be down as soon as possible with Fontaine."

"You have to torture that bitch, John. The Eagle has to send her straight to hell but not before a long, long torture session."

"I promise she will suffer in unimaginable ways. Now, take Sam down to the truck. I will be down soon."

Jim lifted Sam's lifeless body into his arms and kissed her forehead as he carried her to the elevator. The Eagle zip tied Fontaine's hands and feet and then began to move through the rest of the condo room by room photographing with his tablet the horror that many of those rooms held.

CHAPTER FIFTEEN

"This nightmare is never over."

John pulled the truck into the lair's underground garage and called for Sara and Karen. Sara came out first, and he asked her to prepare operating room one. She walked away, and Karen asked, "Have you spoken to Sam? Sandy is beside herself."

"Sam is dead." Karen stood with a stunned look on her face. "Her body is in the truck along with that of her killer. I have to collect one other person. I need you to stay with the body and Jim. Please call Jade and Jessica and ask them to come over."

Chris walked out into the garage as Jim lifted Sam's covered body from the back of the truck. He didn't say anything, but when he moved to take Sam, Jim yelled, "No! The killer is in there. Grab that bitch and take her to operating room one. John, I'm going to lay Sam to rest in operating room three. You will have to get Hampton yourself. I have to call Sandy."

As he walked slowly into the lair, he passed Karen and then Sara. Karen was crying, and Sara asked, "Who is in the blanket?"

"Sam, Sara. It's Sam. I don't know any details other than John says she's dead and has asked for Jade and Jessica to be called."

Sara ran to John and grabbed him by the arms. "What the fuck happened?"

"Sam got drunk and went after the killer on her own and got herself killed."

"And you couldn't save her? That's your fuckin' job, John. It's what the Eagle does."

"I can't save people from themselves, Sara. She made a move that I could not have anticipated. Sandy called me frantic while Jim and I were with Bailey Black. She told me that Sam had a lot to drink and toasted her own death then left Santiago's, and we found her, but it was too late. I still have one more person to grab before this nightmare is over."

Sara had tears running down her face. "This nightmare is never over, John. It's never over."

Beverly was working when her office phone rang. When she answered, the line went dead and someone hung up. She looked at the clock on her computer and saw it was after ten p.m. She started to put papers in her briefcase along with her tablet when a disembodied male voice called her name.

"Ms. Hampton." The office was dark but for her desk lamp, and Beverly screamed at the sound. She felt around on her desk and pressed a button and more lights came on in her office. The Eagle was seated on a couch in the middle of her office, his dead eyes staring at her.

"Jesus Christ! Who the hell are you?"

"What's in a name, Ms. Hampton? Is it really important at this moment?"

"Who are you? How did you get in here?"

"Joann Fontaine is in my custody, Ms. Hampton, and I know her cruelty."

Beverly began shaking, "You're the Iron Eagle?"

"Yes, I am, and you're an accessory to murder."

"I told Joann that she was playing with fire."

"She did play with fire, and she is now getting burned. You played with fire, too, Ms. Hampton, and now it is time that you pay for your sins."

"I don't deserve this. I did what I had to to stay alive. Joann is a nut job. I have known her for years. She would have killed me."

"Why didn't you go to the police if you felt your life was in danger? Why did you feed her depravity? What was in it for you? You bear responsibility for those who are dead; you helped her."

"I didn't want to die. I didn't want to believe that she was doing what she was doing. It was all fantasy so many years ago. I was an impressionable kid when I met her. She introduced me to a new type of sexual lifestyle, one that I enjoyed. I could never have imagined that the years would lead down this road."

"I saw the bodies hanging in a cooler in her condo, Ms. Hampton. I saw the machine she used to tear her victims apart. I have seen the blood eagle tattoo on her back. I have been told of her obsession with me, her fantasies about me, yet she has yet to formally meet me."

"I don't understand. You have Joann, but she doesn't know it?"

"That's correct. I was too late to save her last victim."

"Her last victim?"

"Yes."

"Who was her last victim?"

"Sheriff Samantha Pritchard, an hour ago. She slit her throat with a sword before I could get to her."

"Then how do you know about me?"

"I didn't know everything. You just furnished me with a quick admission, Ms. Hampton. Those quick to protect their personal interests often betray themselves just as you have done." The Eagle pulled out a tablet and sat it on a table in front of the couch with the screen facing Beverly. She could see Joann nude on a table in a brightly lit room with an IV; her eyes were closed.

"Is she dead?"

"Not by a long shot, now there are two ways that we can do this. You can confess here and now to your involvement with Ms. Fontaine and tell me the whole truth for the record, and I will end you quickly."

Beverly started crying. "Or?"

The Eagle pressed a button on a small remote, and a video of one of his victims played for Beverly to see. A man screaming, his body cavity open, and his organs being removed while he was being kept alive. Beverly started to heave and in a matter of seconds she was vomiting on the floor. "Or you can endure what Ms. Fontaine is going to endure and so much more. I'm a master at torture, Ms. Hampton. I can keep my victims alive for days, weeks, even months. The animal you see before you is enduring what I call a living autopsy. It took hours, and he felt every cut of my blade. I later put him on a heart lung machine after removing all of his organs just to keep his brain alive, so I could do even more things to him that even Ms. Fontaine could never imagine. So, this is your fate if you refuse to cooperate."

"I don't want to die."

"You chose to commit these crimes. You must pay for them."

"But I didn't kill anyone." The Eagle sat back on the couch and pulled a tranquilizer gun from his body armor. "Is that the fast way that you spoke of?"

"No."

"But it's a gun."

"It fires tranquilizer darts. It's how I subdue my prey before taking them back to my lair where Ms. Fontaine is now."

"If I choose the fast way, what happens?"

"You will have to cooperate to find out, but I can say you will avoid the fate you see going on before you at my hands."

Beverly started talking. She began with the first time she met Joann and continued up to the present day. She explained everything she had done and all the people that she helped Joann get and kill, including

Steven Black and Kristy Yates. It was ten after one when she finished, and she sat at her desk trembling and crying through the whole confession. When she was finished, the Eagle thanked her.

"You have put all of the pieces to this puzzle in place, Ms. Hampton. Some say that confession is good for the soul."

"Confession isn't going to save me, is it?"

"No. I'm afraid not, but it must feel good to know that you have let me know all of the evil that Ms. Fontaine committed. Her obsession with angels is fascinating to me. She saw her blood eagle torture as a way of creating angels out of those she felt were less than human. It always perplexes me when people see themselves in a light that makes them superior to their fellow man. Joann Fontaine is a monster, and you helped that monster get what she needed to stay off law enforcement's radar. Had it not been for the public killings she did over the past several days, and the survival of a federal employee's child who she tortured, her deeds would have remained secret, and you two could still be doing these savage things. But, alas, you have told me the impetus for these two killings, and it was simply money. Money. The downfall of so many, not just animals like you and Ms. Fontaine, but everyday people so blinded by the desire for the material that they will lie, cheat, and even kill to get what they want. It still amazes me after all of these years."

Beverly sat still at her desk as the Eagle put his tablet back in his armor as well as his gun. He pulled a syringe out of a pocket and sat it on the table. "What is that?"

"The manner in which you are going to die."

She fell to the floor crying and begging as the Eagle rounded her desk, grabbed her by the back of the neck, and drug her across the room. He placed her on the floor in front of the table. The clear syringe with a light blue-green fluid in it sat on the table with a cap on the needle.

"What is that?"

"It is the manner of execution for you."

"But I don't want to die. Please. I have answered everything. Take me to jail. I will plead guilty. I have confessed everything."

"A waste of time, Ms. Hampton. You don't deserve the time of a judge and jury. You don't deserve to grandstand and change your mind once in custody. No. This is the fate you deserve."

"You said it would be fast."

"By my methods of torture, it will be incredibly fast." The Eagle picked up the syringe, removed the cap on the inch and a quarter needle, and plunged it into Beverly's upper arm. She howled as the fluid was injected and then flung herself back on the floor, arching backward and screaming and writhing in pain. The Eagle watched for several minutes as Beverly struggled to breathe, as her eyes shot open in sheer agony. She tried to stand only to fall to the floor. She tried to move only to find her limbs getting rigid from spasms and pain. She was able to eke out, "You said it would be fast…"

"I did, but I didn't say it would be painless. You have hours of this left. You won't appear dead until near sunrise. The paralysis will continue to overtake you until you can only stare at the ceiling in agony. You'll be discovered later this morning by the first person to visit your office. They will call 9-1-1 and then the police will be called in. When the police are called, guess who else gets a call?" Beverly was frothing at the mouth as the muscles in her legs contorted against her bones. The Eagle unzipped the back of his mask and removed it. Beverly's eyes went even wider, but she was unable to speak.

"I will be called to this scene as well, Ms. Hampton, in my capacity as the Deputy Director of the FBI. I will be the one who takes over the investigation into your death or what looks like your death. You see, the drug that I have administered will render you dead to the very, very untrained eye, but you won't be dead. You will be catatonic with no discernable pulse or respiration. The coroner will be called in. You might have heard of the heads of the Los Angeles Medical Examiner's Office, Doctor Jade Morgan and Doctor Jessica Holmes. They work closely with me, and they will treat you as dead and transport you to the morgue where you will get your final end on their autopsy table."

John stood and put his mask in his pocket and rolled Beverly onto her side as she convulsed. "I must leave you now. I will see you later. Enjoy your death. I know I'm going to." He paused then took her face in his hands and looked into her wide eyes. "I almost forgot. I won't get the opportunity to say these words in front of everyone else, but may God not have mercy on your soul, Ms. Hampton."

With that, he dropped Beverly's head on the office floor as drool pooled around her head. She was losing the ability to move, and he looked at a clock on her desk and saw it was after three a.m.

"Well, I'm off, Ms. Hampton. I have to deal with Ms. Fontaine. I must see that much harm comes to her."

Jim was sitting in the operating room with Sam's body when Cindy arrived. She didn't say anything. She walked up to Sam and put her hand on her face and stroked it. Jim was stooped over on a stool, and Cindy said, "You need to sit in a chair, Jim."

"I don't want to leave her alone."

"Has Sara been in to check on her?"

"She died in my arms, Cindy. She died in my arms."

Cindy stood with her hands on his shoulders. She looked down at the dried blood on his pants and shirt and at Sam's peaceful face. "Did she say anything before she died?"

"She saw Maria. I don't know what was said, but she was going with her."

"Sandy is beside herself, according to Karen. She doesn't know where Sam is or what has happened."

"I'm not really worried about fuckin' Sandy at this moment, Cindy. My partner, my friend, my responsibility lies dead here. I thought that losing Steve Hoffman was hard, but it was nothing like this. He was sick. He died a hero. Sam died a hero, too." He paused and took a deep breath. "Why the fuck did she have to go after that bitch drunk? Jesus Christ. She had to have known how dangerous she was. Fuck!"

Jim had been talking, unaware that John was standing in the doorway. "She did what she felt she had to do, Jim."

Jim looked up and saw that John was still in the Eagle's body armor. "Hampton?"

"All but dead, still suffering agonizing pain."

"So, you didn't bring her back here?"

"She confessed. I got everything I needed from her. I don't need the distraction as I deal with Fontaine."

"So, she just dies and gets off easy?"

"She will die, but I wouldn't say that she is getting off easy. I injected her with a new form of Deliverance that Sara and I have been working on. It is an agonizing paralytic. She will have no discernable pulse or heartbeat when found and will die at the hands of Jade and Jessica on the autopsy table."

"Jesus. Do they know about the drug?"

"They helped to perfect it."

Jim laughed. "Shit! With that drug who needs the Eagle's torture? They will feel every cut of the blades and the coroner's saw."

"Exactly. It allows me to send those I don't want in my lair to their deaths in the most agonizing way possible without me having to do the heavy lifting." He walked over to the table and looked at Sam on the bed. "I don't think I have seen that kind of peace on that beautiful face since I have known her."

"I failed her, John. We failed her."

"No, we didn't, Jim. We got there too late to save her, but we were able to keep her from enduring what Kristy and others have endured at Fontaine's hands. I walked the condo, and the woman is a twisted freak, Jim. She blood eagled people thinking she was creating angels. She tortured men and women alike, most of them street people, homeless, prostitutes. Hampton helped her get her prey and had it not been for Fontaine's screw up with Yates, she would still be committing her crimes."

"How do we deal with Sam, John? She died a hero, but this isn't like what happened to Steve. We have no crime scene to stage her body at."

"There doesn't need to be a crime scene to make her a hero, Jim."

"What are you thinking?"

"She died in the line of duty, Jim. She died in uniform doing her job. We can't tie her to Fontaine or Hampton, but we can tie her to being killed investigating the Black killing as well as saving the Yates girl."

"How the fuck are you going to do that?"

"I will handle it, but I will need her body, and I will need it in a few minutes."

Jim looked at Sam and then John and asked, "What about Sandy?"

"We will tell her of the death before it makes the news. Sam will get full honors as a fallen commander."

CHAPTER SIXTEEN

"Let's make Sam a public hero."

Kristy Yates was standing next to her bed after walking around her room with the help of her mother. Sara had been watching her and was happy with her progress. Once Liz got her back in bed, she asked Sara, "When can we safely go home?"

"Soon. The threat has been eliminated, but Kristy still needs observation and physical therapy and will for some time. She also will need a lot of reconstructive surgery, Liz, and as soon as she is well enough, we want to get started on that."

"Her abdomen and chest are healing up pretty well. Thank God that monster didn't hurt her face."

Sara nodded. "I thought the destruction to her abdomen was worse than it was, but it really isn't that bad. In fact, the real work will be on her breasts."

Kristy had been listening to the conversation and asked, "If I'm going to get new breasts, I want big ones."

That got a laugh out of both of the women, and Kristy grimaced a little as she laughed along with Sara and Liz.

It was just before seven a.m., and Beverly's assistant arrived for work. She was putting her stuff on her desk when she noticed a light on in Beverly's office. She walked down the hall and peeked into the office and saw that all of Beverly's things were on her desk, but she didn't see her. She called out, but there was no response, and as she entered the room, she could see Beverly's feet on the floor in front of the small table. Once she rounded the corner, she screamed and called 9-1-1.

John and Jim had taken Sam's body back to her home and had set up a crime scene that was gruesome. John had created a file and loaded it onto a flash drive that would be connected to the discovery of Beverly's body and with a little computer wizardry was able to build a scenario where Sam had an altercation with Beverly at her home over her investigation into Black Robotics that ended in her death. Jim looked over the scene and the placement of the drive and asked, "Who is going to discover the body?"

"LAPD after a 9-1-1 call to check a disturbance at Sheriff Pritchard's home."

"How do we control the media?"

"We don't. We allow this to run the usual investigative course. LAPD will arrive on scene. Once they know it's Sam, they'll call in the sheriff's department and you, and you will tie back to the FBI, and we will go from there."

"So, she was ambushed in her own home?"

"Yes, for her investigation of Black Robotics and her discoveries that had not been released to the public. I already have been notified that Beverly Hampton's body has been discovered, and Jade and Jessica are on scene."

Jim looked down at Sam's face and then the scene, shook his head, and said, "I wish she were here, John. I can't believe this has happened."

"Jim, this is the best we can do for her. She will get the recognition she deserves as a fallen officer and for her service. You, as her undersheriff, will be charged with investigating her murder, but you will also become the Sheriff of Los Angeles County and be sworn in. You know that, right?"

"Yes. It's the least of my fuckin' worries right now. You have to call Sandy before this breaks."

"As soon as the 9-1-1 call is made, I will call Sandy. Now, let's get out of here. I still have Fontaine to deal with as well as the Hampton crime scene."

"Fontaine can wait. You can keep her alive as long as you like. I want a piece of that bitch, John. You're not the only one who is going to extract revenge on her."

John put his hand on Jim's shoulder. "I will not let you down, Jim. You will have your opportunity with her. There is also the matter of the scene at Fontaine's condo. There are at least four bodies hanging in a cooler in her torture room, and there were two young women that I sedated and left in a bedroom who appear to be slaves."

"Jesus Christ! This bitch was doing all of this killing undercover?"

"Yes, now let's make Sam a public hero."

Jade and Jessica were on scene with Beverly Hampton's body when John and Jim arrived. Beverly's eyes were open, and John looked her in the eyes as he spoke to Jade. "So, what do we have?"

"EMTs were called after this one was found unresponsive by her assistant."

"Do you have any theories on the cause of death?"

"Hard to say. She's young. She's been dead for less than an hour. Her body temperature is near normal." Jade pointed to a meat thermometer sticking out of Beverly's liver.

"So, no foul play?"

"I will know more when we get her on the slab and do the autopsy as well as tox screenings."

"Would you do me a favor? We have an interest in this death. Can you do the autopsy this afternoon?"

Jade and Jessica smiled at each other, and then Jade smiled at John. "Of course, Director. We will get her opened up as soon as we get her back to the lab."

"Great. Thank you, Jade. It's important to me to know what might have killed her."

John was looking into Beverly's eyes the whole time he spoke.

When he stood up, Jessica leaned into Jade who was leaning right over Beverly's head and asked, "Did the Eagle use that new Deliverance on her?" Jade nodded, and Jessica looked into Beverly's eyes, smiled, and said, "You can hear me, and you have no idea what we are about to do to you, but it is going to be a horrific way to die."

Jade called out to two of her techs, "Bag this one up and get her back to the morgue. We need to autopsy this one this afternoon for the FBI."

Sandy was at her desk at the FBI headquarters when John called. After hearing his voice, she asked, "John, where are you?"

"I have been bouncing between several crime scenes this morning."

"Do you know anything about Sam? I have been trying to reach her all night."

"Yes, I do. Sandy, are you sitting down?"

"No, John. No, no, no!"

"I'm sorry, Sandy. Her body was found at her home about an hour ago. She was ambushed and killed last night. We're still trying to seal off the scene."

Sandy let out a yell so loud that others in the office came running to her, and she collapsed on the floor in a heap, dropping the phone. One of the agents in the office picked up the phone, and John told him what had happened and asked them to comfort Sandy until he could speak to her in person.

"I'm sorry, Jim. This is a mess of a scene. It looks like Sam put up one hell of a fight even after her throat was slit," the young LAPD officer said as Jim stood in the middle of Sam's living room over her body.

"She obviously fought her attacker. Who found her?"

"We got a 9-1-1 call of a disturbance. We were dispatched on the call. We had no idea that this was Sheriff Pritchard's home, Jim."

"What forced you to make entry?"

"I could see her feet through the glass on the front door and what looked like blood on the walls, so I broke in and found her. As soon as I identified her, I called your office."

Jim stepped back and called out to the EMTs and other officers on scene, "Ladies and gentlemen, this is not just any crime scene. This is the Sheriff of Los Angeles County. I want my CSI team and the FBI's teams on scene as well as Jade Morgan and Jessica Holmes. Please leave me alone with Sam."

The people in the house began to file out and lined the pathway leading up to Sam's home. John and Chris pulled up at the same time as Jade and Jessica in their van. No one spoke, and the LAPD and sheriff's personnel as well as EMTs stood at attention as the four made their way into the house.

Jim was standing near the front door and handed John the flash drive, which he slipped into his pocket. Jade and Jessica made busy work around Sam's body, but they didn't disturb her as they would on any other scene. When her CSI team arrived, she allowed them to photograph the scene and take the necessary information they needed and then she asked them to leave. Word of Sam's death spread fast through the city, and while John and Chris along with the others worked in the house, they had no idea of the growing ranks of local, state, and federal policing agencies that were gathering on the street outside of Sam's home.

John and Chris were talking off in the dining room of the house as Jade and Jessica ordered Sam's body bagged and the familiar red velvet blanket draped over her after she was placed on the gurney. John and Chris came back into the room as Sam's body was about to be moved out of the house. There was a knock on the front door, and Jim answered it to find a teary-eyed young sheriff's deputy holding a neatly folded American flag in his hands which he handed to Jim.

"This is for Sam's body, Jim." He stepped back, and Jim closed the door then took the flag and the six of them unfurled it and laid it over the blanket then opened the door to wheel the body out of the house. Jim looked out the front door as he led the small group with Sam's body to the van and saw a sea of uniforms and cars on the street outside. Jim stood straight and walked out with John and Chris behind him, then Jade and Jessica rolled Sam's flag draped body outside. All of the people around the house stood at attention and saluted as Sam's body was rolled down the walkway to the waiting van.

There were several news helicopters circling the area along with local PD and sheriff's department choppers. Jade put Sam's body in the van and as it began its journey to the coroner's office, a sea of patrol cars escorted the van carrying the fallen sheriff as fellow officers stood on the street as far as the eye could see, saluting.

Jim was in his cruiser followed by John and Chris. Chris was staring at the outpouring of emotion from Sam's fellow officers and others and said, "How sad, John."

"Indeed."

"In order to get a show of respect, Sam had to die."

"She was respected in more ways than you know, Chris, and this is only the beginning of the mourning period for all of the departments." John pulled out his cellphone and called his office. His secretary answered, and he asked her to turn the television monitors at headquarters to a local news station.

Sandy was in one of the breakrooms with fellow agents when the TV was turned on, and she and the agents watched the procession as Sam's body was being escorted to Jade's office.

A news announcer in one of the helicopters was speaking. *"We don't know the circumstances surrounding the death of Sheriff Samantha Pritchard at this time, but the streets and freeways are lined with people and police as her body is being escorted to the Los Angeles County Coroner's Office. One source who wished to remain anonymous due to the ongoing investigation told me that Sheriff Pritchard died valiantly trying to break a serious murder case and that she fought an attacker in her home whom is believed to have been involved in the case. We will keep you updated as information is released by the sheriff's department as well as the FBI, who, we are told, are involved in the investigation."*

Sandy sat staring at the screen and the video of the streets, bridges, and overpasses of the 101 Freeway that were lined with both civilians as well as law enforcement, fire, and EMTs, saluting. She smiled through her tears. "You are my hero, Sam. You are the city's hero, too."

Her fellow agents were all teary-eyed as well as the van pulled into the parking lot, and the flag draped gurney was removed, leaving a sea of people behind.

Bailey Black watched the precession for Sam on a TV at the post office. She stood staring at the screen as tears rolled down her face. Several of her fellow carriers were watching as well. One of them asked, "Did you know her?"

"No. I met her, but I didn't know her."

"Then why the water works?"

"She died doing her job, protecting our city. I have the utmost respect for law enforcement, so this upsets me."

The young oriental man who had asked the question laughed. "If you ask me, good riddance. One less cop to harass or kill one of us."

The outcry against him was loud and immediate, and he tried to skulk out of the room only to be grabbed by a supervisor and escorted to human resources.

CHAPTER SEVENTEEN

"It was all about money, John."

Sam's blood pooled on the floor in Fontaine's condo. The building was crawling with officers, several were hanging over a balcony throwing up after having been in the cooler where the bodies of Fontaine's victims were hanging. Two young women were seated off in a corner of the dining room where they were being interrogated. John entered the room and asked the detectives grilling the two girls to leave.

"What the fuck, Swenson? How did this become the Bureau's case?"

"It's always been the Bureau's case, detectives, now get out of my crime scene and take your puking officers with you. We need men and women with strong stomachs and even stronger investigative skills to deal with this."

"Fuck you. You might be second in command at the Bureau, but we take our orders from headquarters and city hall."

"You take your orders from me, and this is the Bureau's case, now get your asses out of here before I have you forcibly removed."

"One of these women claims to have seen a man in black in the condo last night along with another man and a woman with Joann Fontaine."

"Then, we will interview them and find out who they might have seen."

"What are you trying to cover up this time, Swenson? I have been on too many cases where you suddenly appear and then we learn later that the Iron Eagle was involved in a case, and we don't get our crack at the son of a bitch."

"The Eagle case is open in all jurisdictions, detective. If you're so damn good at your job and have been looking for the him, why the hell haven't you caught him?"

Those words brought silence from the older man. John stared at the two detectives as Jim entered the room. One of the women reacted to Jim's presence, and the detective picked up on it right away.

"Do you know him?"

The young woman looked at Jim but shook her head. Jim walked in and asked why the two detectives were still on scene. John told him they were being smart asses. Jim looked around the room and then at the detectives and said, "Detectives Morrison and Garcia, what a fuckin' surprise. You two want to tangle with Director Swenson and me?"

"What are you doing here, O'Brian? Isn't your boss on the slab at the coroner's office?"

Jim leaped forward and punched Morrison in the face, knocking him to the floor. "You show some goddamn respect you son of a bitch." Jim had his arm pulled back and his hand in a fist.

Chris grabbed him and pulled him back as John grabbed Morrison by the jacket and lifted him to his face. "You get your ass out of my crime scene, or I will start an investigation into the two of you that will make a colonoscopy without sedation sound like a dream." He didn't drop Morrison right away, and the five-foot six detective hung with his feet nearly a foot off the floor.

Jim said, "You better do what he tells you, Morrison. You've already insulted our dead sheriff and pissed me off, now you have Director

Swenson in your face, and believe me, he is the last person you want on your case. He can make your life a living hell."

John still had the shaking man in his grip as Garcia stood up and asked him to put Morrison down. John moved his head slowly in Garcia's direction, and the detective visibly shuddered. "If I see either one of you again on a federal crime scene, you will be living in a mission and eating on food lines. The Sheriff of LA County has been murdered, and you have the audacity to crack wise?" He looked into Morrison's eyes once more and said, "You have now made my list, detective, and you should know mine is not a list you EVER want to be on." He threw the man to the floor, and the two men scurried to the elevator while yelling for all of the LAPD's officers on scene to enter the elevator with them.

Morrison looked at John once he had all of his men on board. "This isn't over, Swenson."

"You're right. It's not. You and I WILL see each other again in a less formal environment. I guarantee it."

Jim was standing next to John as the elevator doors closed. "I have known Morrison and Garcia for two decades. They're dirty cops."

"Well, you know what happens to dirty cops, Jim. You get me the evidence, and they will come face to face with the Eagle."

Once the men were out, Chris asked, "What about the security tape from the lobby and the building? It's going to show Sam entering the building, and she had to have talked to someone at the front desk in order to get up here."

"It's to our advantage. I want you to request the videos and speak to the staff who were working last night."

"And what do you want to know?"

Jim looked at Chris. "For fuck's sake, do you need a goddamn map? Just question them as you would in any other case. Sam was here. John's tied her murder to Hampton, who was one of Fontaine's closest assistants. Sam's presence here will only bolster the case that Hampton was Sam's killer."

"But she wasn't. And what about Sam's car?"

"I took care of it, Chris. It was parked out of the camera's range. Sam knew what she was doing. I drove it out of here hours ago, and it is at her house. Just deal with the employees and the tapes. John will take care of the rest."

Chris left the condo, and John led Jim into Joann's torture room. Jim walked the room with him. There were three Dobermans chained up and muzzled in a corner, and the two men walked into the cold room where the bodies were hanging.

"Oh, for Christ's sake! What a fuckin' mess."

"We need to get our teams in here to seal the scene and remove the bodies. The cause of death won't be hard to determine."

Jim looked around at the bodies hanging from the steel cable running along the ceiling. "What the fuck is this?"

"According to notes on the robotics equipment, this room is what Fontaine called the 'Angel making room.'"

"Angel making?"

"The blood eagle has also been called a blood angel. When the lungs are pulled out and inflated, they appear like seraphim wings."

"Seraphim? You mean angel wings?"

John nodded. "This monster was taking human beings and turning them into her version of angels. I have seen a lot of twisted cases in my career, but this one takes killing and cruelty to new levels."

"So, what now?"

"My people will be here any minute, so we'll turn the scene over to them. I think it's time that the Eagle paid Joann Fontaine a visit to dispel her fantasies about him once and for all." The two men walked to the elevator where John's CSI team and Jade and Jessica were standing. "You will find four bodies mutilated in the back room of the condo in a temperature-controlled room along with several dogs and robotic equipment. Process the scene. Jade and Jessica, the cause of death will be easy to determine. Call me when the autopsy is completed on Ms. Hampton."

Jade nodded. "Will do. We have had one hell of a busy day with multiple bodies and scenes, so it will be later this evening before we can do the exam, but we will call when it's completed."

Sara and Karen were sitting in the lair's foyer having lunch when John, Chris, and Jim walked in. The two were quiet, and Jim asked, "Where is Cindy?"

Sara swallowed some food and said, "I sent her back to work. There is nothing for her to do here." John sat down as did Chris and Jim. "Would you guys like some lunch? I excused the staff and made some sandwiches and salad. You have to be starving."

"I have to deal with Fontaine."

"Not on an empty stomach, John. I know you are going to spend a lot of time with her, but you need to keep up your strength. You all do." Sara got up and left the room and came back with a platter of sandwich meats, rolls, and condiments as well as a bowl of salad, and the three men ate and drank bottles of water in silence.

When the food was consumed, John asked, "How is the Yates girl?"

"She is doing very well. She can go home if you will allow it."

"Just sedate them, and Chris can drive them home. You're sure the girl is okay to be out of the hospital?"

"Yes. The adhesive glue has fused her bone well. She is in good shape but will need to take it easy for a few more days. She should be able to start rehab next week as well as the long process of putting the rest of her body back together."

"How is she handling it?"

"With a real sense of humor, if you can believe that. She doesn't remember much about the attack, but she is a real trooper."

John looked at Chris. "I'm sorry if I have been short with you; it's been an emotional day."

"It's been that way for all of us, John. I will take care of Kristy and Liz, then I think I should go back out to Fontaine's condo and oversee the investigation, so you aren't missed so much."

John nodded and finished his water. Sara stood up and said, "Come with me, Chris. I will sedate the two women and help you get them to the car. Will you be able to get them home without a problem?"

"They are both small. I can carry them without a problem. I think that Kristy's bedroom is still a bloody mess, though, so she will need another room."

"I will talk to Liz and see what she has before I put them under."

The two walked off into the lair's hallway, and Karen sat back and looked at Jim and John. "You two look like hell."

Jim pulled a cigarette out of his top left pocket and lit it as he walked out onto the deck. "Well, I'm glad for that. If I looked good after the past twenty-four hours, I would be damned worried."

"Is there anything I can do for you, Jim?"

"No. There is nothing anyone can do for me." Just then, Jim's cellphone rang. He answered then said, "Yes, Mr. Mayor. I see. I will accept the duties of the sheriff of the county until the election, sir." There was another pause, and Jim spoke sternly, "I will accept the job, Mr. Mayor, but I don't want a single news crew or camera there. Just swear me in and let me go. I don't want anything to take away from the sacrifice that Sheriff Pritchard made for this great city and county, am I clear?" There was a further pause, then Jim said, "Fine. I will be at your office in the morning."

John looked at him. "Are you okay with this?"

"No!"

"But you're going to do it?"

"It's what I do, John. It's what Sam would want me to do, but I have time right now, and I want to be with you as you deal with Fontaine."

John nodded, and Jim flicked his cigarette off the deck and followed John to operating room number one.

Joann was nude, asleep, and strapped to a gurney. John checked the monitors, and her pulse, respiration, and blood pressure were good. The two men went into a side room and put on blue coveralls and then entered the operating room again. John pulled out several syringes from a drawer and injected them into Joann's IV. She jolted awake and looked at the two men, confused at first, and then asked, "Director Swenson, Undersheriff O'Brian?"

"No, Ms. Fontaine. Sheriff O'Brian is now literally acting as the Sheriff of LA County. I am not operating in my capacity with the FBI either. I am acting in my capacity as the Iron Eagle."

"It's you? You're the Iron Eagle?"

"Yes, I am."

"Have you seen my work? Have you seen the angels?"

"Yes."

"Aren't they beautiful? Haven't I done well cleaning the streets of the riff raff? Imagine what we can do together. Imagine how our love will flourish as we work together to clean up the streets of LA. You with the criminal element and me with the dregs of society."

"Those dregs were living, breathing, human beings."

"No, no. Don't you see it? Don't you see how I took the ugly and made them beautiful?"

John had switched on the monitors and recording equipment in the room. "What about Steven Black and Kristy Yates? They needed no transformation. Why did you brutalize them, Ms. Fontaine?"

"Joann. Please call me Joann. May I call you John?"

"Answer the question, Ms. Fontaine."

"Steven and I had a sorted history. He only knew me as his mistress. He didn't know my face, but he knew my tattoo."

"So, he saw it recently and remembered you?"

"Yes, sadly. I liked Steven a great deal. He was good to me."

"So, I understand. There were several blind stock transfers that were to benefit you upon his death."

"True, but that's not why I killed him. He saw the tattoo. He could tie me to the dungeon from years ago. His obsession with me was growing out of control. I felt that I had to act."

"So, Ms. Hampton seduced him and brought him to you?"

"How could you know that?"

"I spoke to her this morning. She was chatty and trying to avoid the fate that awaits you. She told me everything. It is unfortunate that you were able to corrupt a child but that doesn't excuse her role in your scheme. What I want to know is why you decided to reveal your killings now? You have been doing this for years. I have been in your torture room and the cooler. I have seen some of your victims. The modified crematorium with the grinder. As the Iron Eagle, I must say I am impressed at your killing techniques and ability to stay underground, but why come out now?"

"Steven pushed me to the edge, and his daughter was growing so fast. I decided that I needed to rid the world of them. They were the last pieces to my wealth and to building my dream home and angel making facility in Bel Air. I also knew that killing Steven would get the Eagle's attention, but I needed Kristy to move the cases into both local and federal jurisdictions. That way I would be able to get your attention, so I could show you both my perfected craft and draw you to me, so we can be together. I had a bit of a scare yesterday."

"A scare? What type of scare?"

"Bailey Black confronted me, and she was so convincing in her threat that I was worried she was the Eagle, and that would have ruined everything."

"How so?"

"I'm not a lesbian, John. I'm straight. The Eagle has always been spoken of in the media as a man, but Bailey really made me question everything. But here you are, you are even more beautiful than I imagined. Those piercing blue eyes, those huge muscles. You are akin to a Greek god."

Jim remained silent as the two spoke. John called out for Sara, who walked into the room in blue coveralls, and Joann tilted her head and looked her up and down then her eyes went straight to Sara's ring finger. "Who is this, John?" she asked.

"This is my wife."

"You can't have a wife. You're mine." Sara smiled and walked over to the table and began pulling out steel trays covered in white cloths and putting bottles of drugs and syringes on another tray as Joann stared in disbelief. "You are mine, John. You and I are meant to be. Can't you see that?"

"No, Ms. Fontaine. I heard about it a few days ago, but my soulmate is preparing the instruments of your punishment, Joann."

Joann began to thrash her head on the gurney and spit at Sara, which prompted her to slap her hard and force a rubber guard into her mouth. Joann was still trying to scream through the guard as Jim walked up to the end of the gurney. The woman was spread eagle, and Jim picked up a pipe wrench and said, "You murdered Sheriff Samantha Pritchard last night." Joann was too busy trying to scream at Sara to notice Jim lift the wrench over his head. "The time for talking is over, bitch. It's time for you to start suffering." Jim brought the wrench down hard on Joann's right ankle, which snapped like a twig. Her eyes rolled back in her head as she drew a deep breath and then made a high-pitched squeal. John and Sara looked on as Jim struck her on her left ankle, sending blood into the air as the ankle separated at the joint.

Sara applied a tourniquet to her left leg to stop the bleeding. Jim looked at Sara and asked, "Where else can I strike her without killing her?" Sara pointed to her hips, and Jim drew back with the wrench and landed two fast clean blows on the right and left of her pelvis, disfiguring Joann and knocking her out. "Wake her up, Sara." She injected solution into Joann's IV, and she shot awake as Jim looked on. "You aren't going to get out of pain that easily."

John stepped up to Jim and took the wrench from him. "You have started her torture. Are you going to stay for all of it?" Jim nodded as Sara stopped the bleeding at Joann's ankle, and John walked up to the gurney. "You seriously miscalculated who I am, Ms. Fontaine, and for that I and the people of Los Angeles will be forever grateful. I don't usually take pleasure in torture and killing, but in your case, I am going to make an exception. You remind me of a killer I dealt with years ago. A serial killer who hunted the Los Angeles River basin for homeless men and women. When he would find his prey, he would do unspeakable things to them then leave their body parts along the basin. His nickname was the Basin River Killer, but his real name was Francis Statler, and he thought a lot like you. He thought that he was cleaning up the city by killing people and then leaving their remains all over LA. He killed with impunity for nearly four decades until he made one fatal mistake that landed him on my radar. Once there, I found him then tortured and killed him extremely slowly. I used his own torture unit to kill him. It took nearly a week. He begged and pleaded and said many of the things you have said about why you kill, but he wasn't happy to meet me like you were. I am pretty sure that you are beginning to regret luring me out, but you have and now you are in my hands."

Sara injected a syringe of Deliverance into Joann's IV, and she started to convulse on the gurney.

"That was a low dose, right?" John asked.

"Oh, yes sir, a very low dose. If you are planning a living autopsy, you are going to want to blood eagle her first, John."

"Indeed. Let's chill her down and set her up with electrodes. I need a full confession before we go further, and I need to know who her victims were."

Jim asked, "SP-117?"

"Of course. We need to get everything we can out of her before we begin to tear her apart."

Sara injected Joann with the solution, and she began to calm down. The three put on face shields, and John removed the mouth piece. "We are going to talk about your victims, Ms. Fontaine. I want to know everything about your victims from your first kill to the murder of Sheriff Pritchard."

"I don't know names. They were brought to me by all types of people over many years. And even if I did know, who cares?"

"I care. Did those who brought them to you know what you were going to do to the people?"

"Only Beverly knew and that was only after she graduated from college and went to work for Black."

"How did you transport your victims to your home?"

"Oh, that was easy. I didn't always live in my condo. I had a house in Topanga Canyon near the village. I had a van that I used to move victims, and over the years I have had slaves who were loyal to me who helped me get my artwork into the van and home."

"The two women at your condo are slaves?"

"Indeed. They have helped with killings but only after I tortured and drugged them myself. You would be amazed at just how effective LSD can be on an uneducated mind."

"No, I wouldn't. So, you never knew the identities of most of your victims?"

Joann laughed. "Why would I care as long as they suited my purposes for art? I didn't give a damn about their names. I am a sculptor, John, a creator of angels. I brought disgusting beasts into my home and then transformed them into the beauty of the heavens. I didn't care if they were young, old, male, or female. None of that matters to me, just the opportunity to take something ugly and filthy and turn it into something majestic. That was always my goal. I have access to the greatest sculptors in history at the library, and I read and learned about their techniques and styles. I read anatomy books, so I understood how to work with the clay of my creations without them dying before I was finished. You don't see the beauty of my work. You don't see what you and I could be together? How could you be married to such a little troll?"

Sara pushed some liquid into Joann's IV that made her scream. Jim laughed, and John looked on. "Of all the monsters the world has known, man is the cruelest of them all."

Sara nodded as did Jim as John spoke those words. "Sara, sedate Ms. Fontaine, then you and Jim meet me in the conference room."

Sara injected Joann's IV with a sedative, and as she drifted off, she smiled and said, "The Eagle will never harm me. He loves me. He knows he loves me."

Sara shook her head and left the operating room and met up with John and Jim. John had taken a seat at the head of the table under the Eagle sculpture, and Jim sat down next to him.

"I'm not going to get the information I would usually get from a killer. Ms. Fontaine is a pure psychopath. She had no regard for her victims. Her only agenda was to get people for her perverted idea of art and then mutilate them. She will shed little light on her victims and since she incinerated them and most likely threw them out with the trash, identification will most likely never be made."

Jim asked, "Then what are you going to do with her?"

"Everything she did to her victims. She isn't going to get off without suffering, but her delusion is so strong and her imagined feelings for the Eagle so powerful she will see Swenson as her killer not the Eagle. She has been able to remain under the radar for so long because she was able to develop trust from her victims."

"It was all about fuckin' money in the end, John."

"Money was her downfall. She wanted Steven Black out of the way for the stock, and she wanted Kristy Yates because she was the last lineage of Black outside of Bailey, who she would've killed sooner or later. Trevor was a means to an end. She wanted him out of the picture to conclude the stock sale, which she has admitted would make her rich. It was her desire for a relationship with the Eagle, however, that brought her killing out into the open."

Sara was leaning on the back of one of the chairs in the room. "There's a trend I see when you get female serial killers as opposed to male."

John nodded. "Go on."

"All of them manage to stay under the radar from law enforcement, and all of them have motives that usually involve money."

"But this one is unique because she started off thinking she was creating art from what she perceived as trash people. She didn't see her victims as human, which is normal for this type of killer. She had the perfect cover as a librarian and a supposed celibate one at that. Her family is wealthy, so money wasn't the driving force behind her killings. I did some research on her background before she took the job as the head librarian for LA and what I discovered was a very well educated and well-traveled Joann Fontaine. She spent her teens and twenties in school and studying and traveling abroad. There is a case in Florence, Italy, that is still unsolved. A fifteen-year-old girl vanished near the Uffizi in the spring of 2002. The police in Florence have been baffled by the disappearance, yet I found the girl."

"You found her?" Jim asked.

"Indeed, I did. The girl went missing on a Saturday. She was a local street vendor and artist who worked the square around the palace with her parents selling their own renderings of the sights of the city and its history. The girl vanished while working. In a report to the police, her parents said the last time they saw their daughter she was speaking to a young woman about a watercolor she had done of the Piazza Duomo, one of the most recognized landmarks in Florence. A week later, in Rome, the body of an unidentified woman had been discovered near the Trevi fountain. The body had been mangled beyond recognition and placed among other statuary in the fountain area. The body had been at the location for nearly a week, and neither tourists nor locals knew that she was not part of the fountain's back artwork. In fact, it was only by accident that she was recovered at all. A worker cleaning the fountain in the early morning hours discovered that the figure was not a sculpture but a human body that had been dunked in plaster after having been mutilated, its lungs pulled up through its back to look like a blood eagle or angel. The two crimes were never connected as the body was so badly decomposed under the plaster that it was unidentifiable. I sent a message through Interpol to authorities and our field office in Rome to get DNA samples from the family. The results are pending, but I'm sure that this was one of Ms. Fontaine's first victims. She had been in the city for three weeks and was there for two more after the girl vanished before moving on to Rome and then to southern Italy and Sicily, before going back to France where she was studying. If the DNA comes back positive, we will have solved one case for a family, but we will never get an admission from Fontaine. She is too far gone."

Jim shook his head as he lit a cigarette. "Just kill her as brutally as possible and let's move on with other more important events, like laying Sam to rest."

"I have plans for her and will start now. Sara, let's flip her onto her stomach and wake her up. Ms. Fontaine is going to experience what it feels like to become one of her angels."

Jade and Jessica were standing over Beverly Hampton's nude body. Beverly's eyes had greyed over, but Jade had the light of the autopsy room bright on her body. She had several of their TV monitors on and in plain sight of Beverly. Jessica looked at her and asked, "So, she's still alive?"

"Yep. John gave her a new type of paralytic that slows bodily function to a crawl but gives the body enough resources to keep the brain alive and aware."

"Jesus! So, she can hear us? She is aware of what is happening to her?"

"Yep. John wanted her opened up like this. She is going to feel everything we do to her but will be unable to react." Jade took a scalpel from the surgical table and made a Y-shaped incision from shoulder to shoulder and then cut Beverly down to her pubic bone. The two worked on getting all of the surface skin open, then Jade called for the bone saw. As she cut into Beverly's sternum, Jessica looked down into the Beverly's dead looking eyes and saw tears flowing down the sides of her head.

"You're right. She can feel everything we are doing. She's crying like crazy."

Jade laughed. "Let's remove her ribcage."

There was no microphone on for the autopsy, only cameras. Beverly could see herself on the screens, and Jessica knew it. She reached in and started moving around organs. "She is still warm. Look at that liver. Very healthy. She must have been a health nut. The heart, too. That thing could be transplanted. All of her viable organs could. It seems a waste."

The two women took their time removing and weighing and reporting on organs while making sure to keep all vital organs intact as they worked. Jessica was working around Beverly's heart when she noticed that it had the mildest of vibrations and then a slight beat. Jessica jumped when it beat hard several times, which made Jade laugh.

"Got you. I told you she was still alive."

Jessica looked into Beverly's crying eyes then back at her internal organs and asked, "How long are we going to keep her alive?"

"It has been long enough. Hand me the skull saw. Let's take a look at her brain and spinal cord."

CHAPTER EIGHTEEN

"Will he be okay?"

"Hampton is dead." Jade said coldly to John over the phone.

"How did she die?"

"Well, after a long autopsy, I opened her skull and pulled her brain and spinal cord out. You should have seen the look on her face."

"Thank you for letting me know."

"How is it going with Fontaine?"

"Sara and I have blood eagled her. She's alert and trying to lash out, but she is helpless to do anything. We have her on her side, and Sara has her opened up and has been removing organs while we help her to breathe with a ventilator."

"Gruesome."

"No more gruesome than what you just did with Hampton."

"True, true. I don't know that Hampton deserved to die as brutally as Fontaine, but she is dead, and she did suffer."

"Fontaine will suffer much longer than Hampton did. We're going to submerge her in a salt bath in the isolation tank. She is going to really enjoy that."

"Ouch! You can also put the bitch on her back because she will float, allowing her to take in air."

"Oh, I plan to keep her in there for several hours with a nice LSD and Deliverance cocktail."

"She brought this on herself. How's Jim doing?"

"Better. Cindy is here at the house, and we are going to have dinner as soon as I have Fontaine in the tank. He has to take the oath of office tomorrow morning, and he's not happy about it."

Jade was quiet for a few seconds then said, "You do know Sam was on a path to death, right?"

"What? Are you saying that she was suicidal?"

"Duh. She has been since Maria's death. She didn't know what to do with herself. She didn't want to be Sheriff or to work in the private sector. I don't know all of what happened with this Fontaine chick last night, but I think that Sam went there knowing that she was going to die."

"I don't want to believe that, Jade."

"Whether you want to believe it or not, I think it is the truth. She will be laid to rest in a few days. Jim will get his shit together, and Jessica and I will go on about our business dealing with the dead. It was exhilarating saving the Yates girl, though, and Sara tells me that she is doing well."

"She is. She's home with her mother. Sara is going to stop in and check on Kristy in the morning."

"Are you ever going to tell her that Steven Black was her father?"

"That's not my responsibility. It's up to her mother, but I see no reason to do it. She didn't know the man. Why add more to the trauma that she endured?"

"I agree. Jess and I are knocking off. It's ten after seven, and we are going to stop at Santiago's and get shitfaced and take a taxi home."

"Just drive home and leave your car. I think that Karen and Chris are planning to have dinner there. Perhaps you four could drive together then have Javier call you two a cab when you're ready to go home."

"Is Chris still there?"

"He was dealing with the Yates women, but he and Karen are both here, so drop off the car and then you guys can drive together over to Santiago's. We have had enough loss to our group for one day."

Jade told him she would and hung up. Jessica was sitting across the desk from her. The room was dark but for a desk lamp. "Do you think we did the right thing with Hampton?"

"Absolutely. She was a killer, Jess, and John didn't want to deal with her, so we did."

"That's not what we do, Jade."

"It's what we did today, and I have no regrets. If you do, then might I suggest you go open locker fifteen and look at the body of Samantha Pritchard to get your mind right."

Joann was floating in a cool liquid, her eyes shooting back and forth in the darkness of the tank. John and Sara had been watching her on the infrared camera in the tank for about thirty minutes. Sara was looking at the EEG that was attached to Joann's head. "She is really freaking out in there. Her BP is one ninety over one thirty, and her pulse rate is near redline at one eighty."

"Do you think she's going to stroke out?"

"She's been in there for eight hours, John. Sooner or later, her body is going to give up."

"I don't want her dead just yet."

"I will administer a light sedative. That will bring her down a bit. I think that we should stop the cocktail and move her out of the tank."

"Agreed. I think it's time to grind on her."

Sara smiled as she injected Joann's IV, and the two watched as her vitals settled. They removed her from the tank and rolled her on a gurney back to operating room one. The industrial meat grinder shined brightly in the operating room lights, and John tied off Joann's thighs with tourniquets as Sara tied off her wrists with a leather strap and put the cherry picker hook between the straps. John used a remote control and lifted Joann off the gurney as she babbled incoherently. Her lungs were still being inflated by oxygen that Sara had set up for her on a moving dolly. The two of them swung Joann over the meat grinder then started the blades.

"You're not sure if this is real or a hallucination, right?" Sara asked.

John began lowering her into the blades and said, "It's no hallucination, and while it will hurt, it won't kill you." Joann's screams reverberated off the walls.

Jim had been out of the operating room while Joann was in the isolation tank and had come back in as her feet hit the grinder. It was loud, and Jim yelled, "This won't fuckin' kill her?" John shook his head. "Just how do you plan to finish her?"

"In the oven on low."

Jim smiled as he looked into Joann's face of agony. "She can't hear us, can she?"

"No. She's focused on the grinding. I will stop the machine just above the knees."

"How are you keeping her organs in?"

"Sara used surgical mesh after we removed most of her organs. The only thing inside is her heart. Her lungs are on her back, and the rest of her organs are in the incinerator."

Once Joann's legs had been ground off, John stopped the machine and moved the cherry picker back over to a steel crematorium table and laid her body on it face down.

Jim and Sara followed John out the side door of the lair to the incinerators, and John pressed the black button that slowly creaked open the steel doors. Joann's head faced the unit, and she tried to cry out but was unable to say anything intelligible.

John leaned down near her face and looked into her terrified eyes. "This is where we part, Ms. Fontaine. You will now be cooked to death before being cremated. I'm not going to lie to you. It will take time. I have the unit set to take in enough air to keep you alive through the heat for at least an hour. It is ironic that we both got rid of our victims in the same manner. Well, I have things to attend to, like cleaning up the last of your mess. As I send you into death, may God not have mercy on your soul."

John and Jim pushed the steel tray into the incinerator. Jim looked through the glass into the incinerator as Sara and John stepped back. He stood there for a few seconds and could hear Joann's screams and cries. He stepped back, turned to John and Sara, and said, "It wasn't enough torture for what that bitch did to so many and to Sam."

"It's never enough, Jim. For the majority of people who I find, no amount of torture is ever enough. The human body can only handle so much before it goes into shock and once that happens the effectiveness of the torture is lost. Joann Fontaine is the worst killer I have ever come across. I have never been face to face with someone so out of touch with reality that even as I worked on her she refused to accept the fact that it was the Eagle killing her not me. She will be dead soon, Jim, and her ashes will go where her victim's ashes went – into the trash. I wish I could extract every ounce of agony out of her, but in the end, there is only so much I can do to the perpetrators of crimes, and there is no way to cover the agony and suffering that she and others have imposed on so many."

Jim nodded. "It's better than the bitch getting the death penalty, a needle, and a nap." Sara spoke up, "Yes, it is, Jim. You have to accept this. As cold a comfort as it is, she suffered unimaginably for her transgressions." The three walked back into the lair, and John and Sara spent an hour cleaning up the machinery and the operating room as Jim helped the best he could. The sun had set, and Jim walked out onto the deck where he lit a cigarette and leaned over the glass railing, smoking. Sara and John were in the foyer, and she asked, "Will he be okay?"

"He will never be the same, Sara. He loved Sam in a way that defies our understanding of love. She was his conscience in a lot of ways, and she was his pupil. He was her protector. He will go on with his life and work, and he will be effective at it, but he won't be the same emotionally."

"Do you think Sam's death will soften him?"

"No. I think it has kindled in him a deeper hatred for killers. I think it has awakened in him the repressed desire for vengeance against the evils he has seen over the course of his career and in working with the Eagle."

"You don't think he is going to become a killer, do you?"

"Not at all, but he will never again equivocate about what to do with the monsters. Whether that is good or bad remains to be seen. For now, all we can do is wait."

CHAPTER NINETEEN

*"We live the loss; we fill the space,
and we work to keep people safe."*

The media had picked up the story of Sam's murder and was running it on every network. Sandy was sitting in Jim's home watching some of the coverage. Law enforcement from across the country and around the world were descending on Los Angeles for the funeral, which was to be held the following day.

"I have never seen such an outpouring of love and compassion," Sandy said to Jim and Cindy, who were sitting in the room with her.

"It's fake, Sandy." Jim said in a snarky way, and Cindy slapped the side of his arm.

"It's not fake, Jim. People respected Sam, and they want to be here to see her off."

"Yeah, well, no one gives a rat's ass when we are out in the field doing the work of law enforcement. No one cares that all of us put our lives on the line for the safety of the public until one of us gets killed.

Then, all the big wigs come out and say their speeches and get their photo ops for whatever purpose it will serve them. There are many who will get a lot of mileage out of Sam's death. The mayor, city council people, local politicians. I've even heard a rumor that President Hernandez is flying in for the funeral tomorrow."

Sandy's eyes went wide. "The President of the United States is coming out for Sam's funeral?"

"That's what I heard."

"Wow! What an honor for Sam."

Jim shook his head. "An honor for Sam? Sam's fuckin' dead, Sandy. She doesn't give a rat's ass who is at her funeral. The fuckin' pope could show up, and she would be none the wiser. The mayor asked me this morning how I was holding up when he swore me in. I just looked at him, shook my head, and walked out of his office. These politicians don't have the first clue of what it takes to keep a city safe. They don't give a fuck about the sacrifices we make every day on the streets of this country or what our military men and women endure to keep this nation safe. They are all two-faced assholes who will come out, say a few words about a woman they didn't even know, then go back to their bullshit. We live the loss; we fill the space, and we work to keep people safe in our roles as peace keepers until the next death."

Cindy had tears in her eyes as did Sandy. Cindy turned off the news and looked at the two of them and said, "Jim is right. I hate to admit it, but he's right. Every word that he has said is exactly what this is all about. The men and women of law enforcement coming in for the funeral understand the loss; they understand the agony of what it is to do what you two do every day to keep people safe. But the rest of this is just political wrangling, and I would guess that the vast majority of those coming here are only doing so because of Sam being the first openly bisexual Sheriff of LA County. They can get some mileage out of being seen as supporting the LGBTQ community, when, in fact, most of them don't care and don't understand the sacrifices Sam made. Jim has told me stories of many a time in a face-off with someone in local law enforcement and his own department where Sam would be openly mocked for her lifestyle and her relationship with Maria. Try doing that job all the while knowing there are people who only want to see you fail. Jim's right. This is a dog and pony show, and he has to eulogize Sam tomorrow while trying to stay as politicly correct as possible." Sandy nodded, and Jim walked out onto the deck, lit a cigarette, and stood looking out at the sea. Cindy looked at Sandy and asked, "How are you holding up?"

"It's hard. We weren't really a couple. We were just testing the waters, but I can't stop thinking about her. She was so full of life and passion, but she was also really sad. She missed Maria. She just couldn't find a way past her death. The first time we made love, she cried for an hour afterward. There was nothing I could do to console her."

"I spoke to her a few times as her friend and as a therapist. She carried a great deal of survivor's guilt. She told me that she and Maria had talked about marriage and that she was brutal with her over the subject. She had a lot of regrets after Maria's death. She confided in me that she had strong feelings for you, however, and that she was trying to reconcile those with the guilt she was carrying."

Sandy sat crying as Jim walked back into the room. "Ladies, nothing is going to get resolved with all of us sitting around here having a pity party. I have work to do, so do you two, so let's get to our offices and get to it, and tomorrow we will see Sam off and try to get our lives back on track."

John was working on the Black case when Chris popped in. "Have you tied up the loose ends on Sam's death and heroics?"

"I will release the final report tonight at a press conference."

"I heard that President Hernandez might fly in for Sam's funeral tomorrow."

"That's right. I spoke to Liz Yates, and she said that she has an advance team from D.C. in her office, and they are working up the President's schedule for tomorrow."

"So, is it just an in and out trip for him?"

"I don't know."

"Does he want to meet with you?" John nodded. "He wants you in Washington, doesn't he?"

"If he wins reelection in November, he has asked me if I would accept his nomination to become his Director of the FBI."

"And what are you thinking?"

"I don't know, Chris. I'm flattered by the offer but pushing papers and overseeing the politics of the Bureau just isn't what I want to do. I didn't want the promotion I have and have delegated off most of that job. The director isn't thrilled that I'm being looked at for the position either, and I don't blame him. He has been with the Bureau for decades and is a good man. Director Collins is a politician whereas I'm not. He knows the ins and outs of state and local affairs. He likes this stuff. I just don't."

"Then turn the President down."

"I wish it were that easy. Even Collins has told me that it is a huge honor that the President is bestowing on me and shows a great deal of trust for both the rule of law and the morale of the agents."

Chris laughed. "If they only knew what you moonlight as."

John sat back in his chair with his arms behind his head. "What if I told you that the President knows I'm the Eagle?"

Chris's eyes went wide open. "The President knows?"

"Sort of. The Eagle saved his life several years ago as well as the country. While my identity was never officially revealed, the President got a look at my face while I was saving him."

"And he has never pursued the situation?"

"It's never come up, but he has put the Bureau's search for the Eagle on the back burner."

"I often wondered why Washington wasn't more active in trying to find the Eagle."

"Well, now you know."

"You're not even on the FBI's ten most wanted list."

"No, but that has as much to do with me as with the Bureau. I manipulate the local list to keep the Eagle off it. There are much more dangerous criminals out there, so I will hopefully never make the top ten."

"There are a few names on that list that the Eagle did away with a long time ago. Why not remove them?"

"It keeps us on our toes. It keeps people looking over their shoulders, and I want that. The general public has no idea the danger they face each and every day just going about their business. There is a killer in all of us, and there are many, many bad people in the world like Joann Fontaine who never make the radar but who kill each and every day. Keeping a few of those reminders up there, like the Basin River Killer, is a good thing. Even though he is long dead, and there haven't been crime scenes in years, he is the boogieman that even in his absence is a deterrent for crime and a warning to the general public to pay attention."

"So, how are you going to handle Sam's funeral tomorrow?"

"I will say a few words. It's Jim I'm worried about."

"Why? Are you afraid he won't hold it together?"

"I'm afraid he will go off on people. He's angry, and the people who pour in who are not in law enforcement and who are using this as a political platform or photo opportunity are going to piss him off, and you have seen Jim when it comes to dealing with the media. Imagine how he is going to deal with a bunch of politicians and bureaucrats who didn't know Sam but are going to get their fifteen minutes before the city, state, and nation. The funeral will make all of the national news networks, so I just hope he holds it together and doesn't start ripping people from the lectern."

CHAPTER TWENTY

She didn't shine a seat with her ass."

The Los Angeles Cathedral was standing room only for Sam's funeral. The venue could accommodate up to three thousand people but had pushed beyond that number as those who couldn't get in stood outside of the cathedral listening to the service on loud speakers. The venue was packed with dignitaries from across the country as well as local, state, and federally elected officials. President Hernandez had delivered an impassioned speech as did others, including some of Sam's fellow deputies. John spoke briefly as was his norm, but he spoke highly of Sam and all she stood for and sacrificed for the city and county of Los Angeles. Sam's flag draped casket lay on a table in the front of the church, and Jim sat with Cindy and Sandy on each side of him as speaker after speaker took their turns addressing the crowd. Jim was to be the last to speak, and he had several folded pieces of paper in his hands as he watched and waited for his turn.

Jim stepped up to the podium that overlooked the thousands of people in attendance. Sam's casket was in front of him, and he looked down at it as he put the papers down and moved the microphone. His uniform was neatly pressed, and the five stars on his collar and his badge shined brightly in the light of the huge hall.

"I have had the unfortunate honor of delivering words at funerals over the course of my career. None sadden me more than a fallen peace officer. Sheriff Samantha Pritchard started off as my understudy in law enforcement and then proceeded to run for office and was elected by the citizens of Los Angeles County. Sam was a remarkable officer. Her passion for public safety was rivaled by none. She kept a cool head in the face of adversity. Her smile could light up a room, and in her moments of anger, she could send a shiver down even the most hardened of officers, myself included." There was light laughter from the crowd. "I have listened to many of you speak, but most of you never really knew her. You're here for your own purposes, political or otherwise, and that's fine, but don't stand here in front of her fellow officers and the officers from around this country who have traveled here to pay their respects and pretend that you knew or even cared about her because you didn't. It was my honor to have served with Sam for three years. It was my honor to have served as her Undersheriff for two of those years and to know a woman of great integrity and care. She was lauded for being the first openly bisexual Sheriff of Los Angeles County. It was, to her, the least interesting thing about her. She didn't care what others thought. She had a job to do, and she did it well. Sam never saw herself as fighting for a cause as a bisexual person. It was just her lifestyle and was as she told me nearly daily, 'Not all of who I am.'

"Sam was a fighter. She fought to make the Sheriff's Department one that drew respect. She held all of us who served under her to a high standard, and she set the bar high and lived what she spoke. There were dark days in recent months after the death of her life partner Maria Martinez. She struggled with her death but kept pushing forward to protect and serve the people. Her passion for police work showed in everything that she did, and she more than a few times put her life on the line to protect not only the public but in many cases her fellow officers. That's the Samantha Pritchard I knew. A sheriff who was unselfish in her duties and at all times worked to better our department and the lives of our citizens. I miss Sam, and I will miss her for the rest of my life. She was an inspiration to me and a role model for others. Every now and then, she would be at a function and a young girl would come up to her to tell her she wanted to be just like her. She would always tell them if they wanted to be a deputy to do well in school and to follow their parents' and teachers' guidance. Most of the men and women in law enforcement here in Los Angeles know me well. They know I don't give false praise, and I'm one for speaking my mind no matter what anyone thinks of it. I'm not politically correct, and I don't apologize for that. I call it like I see it, and in the case of Sam … she was someone I could depend on twenty-four-hours a day, seven days a week. We lost a lot of sleep working cases. She wasn't a sheriff in name only. She was a sheriff in action. She didn't shine a seat with her ass or run around to political rallies. She was on the street doing police work, investigating cases, and getting her hands dirty while working to keep this city safe. So, to all of you who sung Sam's praises today and knew her, thank you. To those of you that are here because it is politicly correct or who plan to use this sad day for your own gain, you can go fuck yourselves. Those out there who put on a gun and badge every day and go out in the streets to protect the people of your communities, thank you for being here and for traveling to be here for Sheriff Pritchard. I know that if she could see this she would be amazed at the outpouring of love and support from her law enforcement family.

"Well, I have said all I feel needs to be said about Sam. We will all follow her body to Forest Lawn where she will be buried and then we will all go on with our lives and duties. We take a brief moment from risking our lives to pay respect to the fallen, then we go back out onto the streets and put our lives on the line to protect people we don't know and that in many cases make our police family a thankless job that few ever really understand. Sam used to ask me why people were so jaded and hateful of police. I used to tell her that it's easy for the general public to vilify us. Some of it we brought on ourselves through the actions of some bad apples, and the rest is just a public that is disrespectful of our duty until they need us and then they hide behind us while we stand in the line of fire. I will miss my friend. I will miss her constant companionship and her zeal for life. I will miss our talks, our time together on duty and off. Samantha was a remarkable woman in and out of uniform. A consummate professional and a genuine person who walked the walk as an example that we all should follow." Jim paused and looked down at the flag draped casket and then the photos of Sam that were posted beside it. He wiped the tears that had built up in his eyes then said, "Godspeed to you, Sheriff Pritchard, and thank you for your service."

The cathedral erupted in applause as Jim finished his eulogy. People outside were applauding, too, and he sat back down as the audience stood and after five minutes of applause the audience became quiet, and clergy said a prayer to close the service. When it was over, Jim, John, Chris, and three other officers took their place on the side of Sam's casket, and the pallbearers carried Sam to a waiting hearse, put the casket inside, and went on to their vehicles. The funeral processional was long, and people stood on the side of the roads and on bridges and overpasses saluting as it went by. The same men removed Sam from the hearse and placed the casket over the open grave. After a twenty-one-gun salute and a few more words from clergy, the flag was removed and folded by the sheriff's honor guard and given to Jim as Sam had no living family.

People started leaving the cemetery, but Jim, Cindy, John, Chris, Karen, Sara, Jade, Jessica, and Sandy remained until the casket had been lowered into the ground. Each took some earth and threw it into the grave. Jim pulled out a cigarette, lit it, and said, "I don't know about you guys, but I could use a drink, and I know just the place." The group walked off, and Jim asked John, "Have you spoken to Hernandez?"

"Briefly before the service."

"Does he still want you to be the next FBI Director?"

"Yes."

"Did you give him an answer?"

"I told him we will cross that bridge when we get to it."

Jim laughed. "FBI Director John Swenson. It has a nice ring to it, don't you think?"

"I said we will cross that bridge when we come to it."

"Yeah, well, that bridge is coming faster than you may think, so you better get your shit together. We aren't politicians, and I know you love being on the street. But there is a need in the Bureau for leadership and accountability that has been lacking. You're the man that can make those changes as America's top cop."

"And the work of the Eagle?"

"At some point the Eagle must die, John."

"And who will protect the people of Los Angeles then, Jim? Who will hold the worst of the worst accountable? My life's work has been to rid society of parasites and as you stated about Sam, I'm not one for shining a seat with my ass. There has to be accountability, Jim, and that's what the Eagle does. He holds people accountable."

"You know there is someone here that can step into the Eagle's role just as others have stepped into the Hudson River Killer's spot. You know who that person is and only you can ordain them to take your spot if you choose to go national."

John stood looking down at Sam's open grave. "The old saying is true. 'No good deed goes unpunished.'"

COMFORTER

The Iron Eagle Series: Book Twenty-Six

PROLOGUE

It was just before sunset, and Jim had been walking the empty rooms of the house that he'd had built for Sam. Cindy had gone into the village to shop, and he was left alone with his thoughts in what was once a promising place. He leaned over one of the decks of the two-story home and looked down at the sand and then out to the sea. The sun was beginning to set, and the air was cooling quickly. He pulled a cigarette from his pocket, lit it, and shook his head as he walked down the back stairs to the beach and over to his own home.

Doctor Brian Cantor had just finished operating on a fourteen-year-old boy who had come into the emergency room of Northridge Hospital with a nearly ruptured appendix. He walked to the waiting room where the family was waiting and reassured them that the young man was going to be fine and then went on break. He walked out onto the back patio of the doctor's lounge, pulled a small vial from his pocket, and popped several pills into his mouth. He shook his head as he swallowed then sat down and closed his eyes to the setting darkness.

Brian had no sooner started to drift off when his sister Beth called his name from the doctor's lounge door. "Brian, are you awake?"

"I am now. I thought you were in surgery."

"I was. My patient tanked. We couldn't get the airway resected. His cancer was far too advanced."

"I'm sorry. Why the hell you decided to go into thoracic surgery I will never know."

"For the same reason that you went into general surgery. We both like puzzles; mine are more controlled, but yours are all over the place."

Beth Cantor walked out into the cool evening, took a deep breath, and asked, "How did it go with the kid?"

"Fine. Routine. He had a hot appendix, but it didn't rupture, so he will be going home by morning. The family was happy."

"Then, all in all it's been a good day?"

"Sure. No one died on my table. For you, what kind of day has it been?"

"Losing a patient is always hard, but I can't work miracles, and he was in his seventies. It was going to be a tough case as it was. I had three other successful operations today, so I would say one loss out of four is a good day. Are you off shift?"

"No. We're short-handed on general surgeons, so Sara asked me to pull a twenty-four hour shift. I'm here all night. What about you?"

"I'm not on staff, so I'm finished for the day. I'm going to go home, run a bath, have a glass of wine, and relax."

"Sounds great. As for me, I'm going to nap here for a few minutes then take a shower in the doctor's locker room and try and grab a few winks before I'm needed."

"Well, I'm off." Beth leaned down and kissed Brian on the forehead and saw the lid on the vial in his pocket. "Jesus Christ, Brian. I thought you were clean."

"What are you talking about?"

"The pill bottle in your pocket."

"It's vitamin B-12 for energy."

Beth grabbed the container and poured several pills into her hand. "Oh, for Christ's sake. B-12, my ass. This is Vicodin. You're using again?"

Brian ripped the bottle out of her hands and put it in his pocket. "I just baby dose to take the edge off the pain in my back. You don't have degenerative disk disease, little sister, so you have no idea what I'm going through."

Beth shook her head. "No, I don't, but I know what happens when you take too much of that shit. You almost lost your license, or have you forgotten the last year? In and out of rehab, patients almost died on your table undergoing routine procedures that every general surgeon could do in their sleep. The hallucinations, the withdrawals. Come on, Brian. Not again."

"I'm fine. I have it under control. My pain is controlled, and I know what I'm doing. I don't care what anyone says. I didn't hallucinate that person stalking the wards."

"There was no one stalking the wards, Brian. You almost got two nurses fired and yourself killed by police, and I know you don't remember that."

"I'm telling you that person stalked and killed people."

"Shit, Brian. People die. For god's sake, you were working on an oncology floor and cardiac floor. No one killed anyone. People die. It's what happens, but you flipped out and swore there was a killer in the hospital. That's when Sara had you placed on a psych hold and when we got to the bottom of your addiction. It was all in your mind, Brian. Sara saved you and your career. If she finds out you're using again, she will fire you and report you."

"I'm fine, Beth. Go home and leave the ER medicine to me."

Beth walked back into the doctor's lounge, and Brian sat back in his chair and stared off into the faintly visible starry sky.

Tamera Jenkins was resting in her bed on the hospital's oncology ward. She had been a healthy happy twenty-five-year-old grad student at Cal State Northridge only a few short weeks earlier and was now fighting for her life. One of the nurses came into the room to check her vitals, and Tammy smiled and asked, "Do you know when I might get the results of the latest blood tests?"

"Oh, they just ran them this morning. It will take a day or two. Just be patient. How's your breathing?"

"Better with the medicine that Doctor Cantor gave to me. I just can't believe I have stage three lung cancer."

"You're a fighter, Tammy. Don't you even start to give in to negative thoughts, sweetheart."

"I'm not. It's just..." Tammy got tears in her eyes, "I was just jogging, something I have done for years, and, all of a sudden, I couldn't breathe. If it hadn't been for a fast-acting coach, I would have died right there on the track at school. I just can't believe how life is normal one minute and the next you're fighting to live, to breathe. It's just not fair."

The nurse forced a smile and patted her on the shoulder. "I've been a nurse for many years, Tammy, and I have seen it all. You're going to beat this. I know you are. Beth Cantor is one of the best thoracic oncologists in the state. You are in the best of hands. Try and relax. Can I get you anything?"

"What I want no one can give me."

"Well, I'm right outside the door. If you need something, just press the call button."

The nurse left the room, and Tammy broke down in tears and sobbed into her pillow.

It was just after midnight when Brian was doing his rounds. His young patient was sleeping soundly, and he read his chart, and everything looked good. He walked the hallway of the hospital ward, room after darkened room, until he came to the oncology wing. He had a patient who had nearly drowned earlier in the day that he had admitted overnight for observation, and the only place that she could get the attention she needed was on the pulmonary care ward in oncology. He pulled his tablet out and began looking up information when he saw a person out of the corner of his eye. He turned quickly in the direction of the image, but it was gone. He walked in the general direction of where he saw the person go and it led down a hall to the ICU. He stopped at the nurse's station and asked if they had been moving around. The three nurses shook their heads, and he smiled and moved on. He walked on to his patient's room and checked her chart, and she seemed to be sleeping fine with no complications. The room was at the end of the corridor near the stairwell, and he scanned the results into his tablet. Once he was sure no one was around, he popped several more pills into his mouth and left the room.

He stopped again at the nurse's station and made small talk then looked over near his patient's room and caught just a glimpse of a person entering the stairwell. He moved quickly in that direction when there was a code blue called out, and he and the nurses on the floor rushed to the patient's room. Brian called for a crash cart and was trying to clear an airway as the nurses administered CPR and were injecting the patient with medications.

"She's in V-fib; I need the paddles." One of the nurses put the conducting gel on the paddles, and Brian rubbed them together, called for a charge, and shouted, "Clear!" He struck the young patient with the paddles, and her body bounced on the bed.

"We're losing her, doctor," one of the nurses called out.

Brian turned up the current and shocked her again, but the arrhythmia was only getting worse. "We need an OR. I need to open her up."

One of the nurses looked down into Tammy's calm face as the monitor began to flatline. Brian was still working on her and had called for a scalpel to open the left side of her chest. He had his hands on her heart and was doing gentle compressions, but the line on the monitor ran flat. After ten minutes, he pulled his blood covered hands out from under the young woman's ribcage and said, "Call T.O.D."

"One fifteen a.m., Doctor Cantor." Brian was handed a towel by one of the nurses and he wiped his hands as Tammy lay dead on the bed.

"Are you the only three nurses on staff here tonight?" Brian asked.

The nurse who had been talking to Tammy a few hours earlier answered, "We are the only ICU nurses here. There are others on the floor, though. Why?"

"Did you see anyone in this room in the past few minutes?"

All heads shook. "No, doctor. There are no visitors allowed right now. I was doing inventory in the back of the nurse's station, and the other two were checking on patients."

Brian looked around the room at the faces staring back at him and then out into the hall. "There was someone else up here. I saw them. I saw them moving in this direction when I entered, and I saw them head down the stairwell just before you called the code."

All three of the women shook their heads, and Angela Sparks, the head nurse and one taking care of Tammy, said, "There was no one else here, Doctor Cantor. I haven't seen anyone all night."

"I want an autopsy performed on this patient."

"You know we can't authorize that. This death will go under review. Sara and Beth will lead it. You can give your input as the attending at the time of death, but all we can do is notify the family and have her body taken to the morgue."

Brian left the room, and one of the other nurses asked Angela, "Isn't Doctor Cantor the one who had a meltdown up here last year?"

"He is."

"Didn't he melt down claiming he was seeing someone in the hospital who was killing patients?"

"Yes."

"Well, you're the boss, Angela, but if I were you, I would wake administrator Swenson and let her know what just happened here."

About the Author

Roy A Teel Jr. is the author of several books, both nonfiction and fiction. He became disabled due to Progressive Multiple Sclerosis in 2011 and lives in Lake Arrowhead, CA with his wife, Tracy, their tabby cat, Oscar, and their Springer Spaniel, Sandy.

CPSIA information can be obtained
at www.ICGtesting.com
Printed in the USA
BVHW030744120620
581315BV00019B/7/J